HIVE

HIVE

VOLUME 1

AMAN

Published by Monastic Hill Studios

Originally published as kindle ebook

ISBN: 978-81-982454-8-9
Kindle Ebook ASIN: B0F2598LGP
Kindle Ebook ISBN: 978-81-982454-5-8

monastichill.com/books

Cover design and illustrations by the author

For my family
where 'exaggerated' storytelling is tradition

For my hometown of Sanchi
which holds a million stories from my childhood

And for you
wherever you are right now

CHAPTER 1

SECOND SON

"**I** found a tooth in my breakfast today!" I told the Devant Priest as I looked down at Solus from the Observatory. He bowed deep as the glow of the great white planet illuminated his pale-yellow scalp.

"Must be the work of some rebellious slave in the Abattoir," the Mandib Devant Priest Ruben, replied with a smile, as he recovered from his insincere gesture of obeisance. I maintained my expression of displeasure to drive home my disappointment. The smug smile faded as he took on a more sincere demeanor.

"I will check with the Foreman and see to it that the slave be punished." Ruben assured me. I did not want him to hurt someone, but cruelty is expected of me, so I kept my mouth shut.

"Don't kill him!" I said hesitantly, as I regretted my words as they left my mouth. The smile on the Priest's face returned.

"As you wish, General!" he spoke with the same smug expression as before. I did not turn my head towards him to maintain the apathetic illusion.

"Has the Emperor talked to you lately?" Ruben enquired.

"No!" I said nonchalantly. The bastard Priest knew this was a tender topic, yet he continued to lead his inquisitions. The memories of my childhood flooded my mind as I raised my arm to dismiss the ambitious Priest.

My name is Zios, General Zios, to be more exact. Me and my brother Agamemnon were born as twins to the Mandib King Atreus of Nenos. The politics of succession began as soon as the midwife carried both of us into the Great Hall. Everyone chose their sides to back either of the two Princes who were difficult to tell apart. It was a zero-sum game of equal odds, and any two opposing courtiers would have begun their machinations as our synchronous cries echoed in the Great Hall of the Royal Palace.

What evaded their feeble, status-driven minds was that me and my brother Agam didn't need words to talk to each other. There was a telepathic bond between us, the existence of which we chose not to share with anyone.

This little telepathic quirk united us as we weathered ceaseless game of thrones, that pitted us against each other in our younger years. We played in the courtyards of the Parthenon in Nenos, and the Gardens of Albany. We reenacted kings of the old as we shared a common love for history and its beautiful ability to predict the future. I never felt alone even when we were sent off to separate masters to learn the art of rule. My brother was always in my ear teaching me everything his Nenoan Grandmaster taught him.

I shared my feelings that I am being trained for priesthood since my master was not Nenoan, rather he was Devant. A man of God, my master taught me how the Devant Religion guides over a million worlds, across multiple galaxies. It was only a matter of time before I realized that my father has decided to go with Agamemnon as his successor and I was being sidetracked.

Agam assured me that this was not the case and that maybe they will switch masters soon and I will be learning more about the Art of War rather than the Birth of Devon on Solus.

I remained suspecting of my father's motives as the conversation between Agam and me, dwindled further and further. I felt alone for the very first time in my life and it terrified me.

* * *

"The Xaracem are on the run!" General Basil's holographic head declared as the Mandib Hussaris stood behind me, intently listening.

"We have managed to corner them in the Bastion of Mount Amperia, you know what this means right?" Basil spoke excitedly.

"I know!" I muttered under my breath as the Devant Priest Ruben sneaked up behind me and move closer to the talking head.

"And so, Devon, the one true Prophet, guided the last of the Mandib to Mount Amperia and saved them from the Great Flood!" Ruben proclaimed as the Hussaris fell to their knees. Their unanimous prostration shook the Nesset Hall aboard our Warship Tigran.

"This is a sign, General!" Ruben approached me as General Basil closed his eyes to pray.

The irony was completely lost on both of these fools. Devon, the founder of the Devant Religion, according to the good book, guided the early Mandib up the mountain to save them from a Great Flood. But now the Xaracem, an alien species was hiding up there, waiting to be annihilated by the modern Mandib.

"Call the Second Sons, we need to account for all eventualities when we attack Mount Amperia!" I ordered Basil as I turned around and made my way out of the Nesset. As I exited the hall, I finally breathed a sigh of relief. The religious nuts always suffocated me. After what felt like an eternity, I calmed down and decided to walk back to the Observatory and look at Solus — the birthplace of my species.

"You must not fail, Brother!" a voice echoed in my mind as I walked the hallways.

"Agam! are you there!" I thought to myself. There was no response.

"Agam! can you hear me!" I spoke out loud this time. I looked around to confirm that nobody saw me. I did not want to get caught talking to myself, while we are on the precipice of something so great.

"Maybe if I take back Solus, Agam would talk to me again" I thought to myself hopefully.

"Or maybe he is just using to me to further his expansionist agenda" a more pragmatic voice called out from deep within. It was true that once our father died, without naming a direct heir, most of the court sided with Agam, to be the next King.

They were right to do so. Agam was so much more qualified to be king. He single-handedly suppressed the Slave Rebellion of Eusebios and managed to bring back our outer colonies back under the rule of Nenos. Me on the other hand wasted my time away in the monastery learning to paint and recite the psalms of Devon. But all of this changed when our Uncle Pittheus attacked Nenos.

* * *

"The Council of Second Sons is now in session!" Ruben declared to a larger Nesset aboard my Nenoan Warship Tigran which was littered with Hussaris and their Generals.

Atop the podium stood seven generals of Devant Warships stationed around Solus. Some were present in person like Basil, Zeno and Demetri while others joined via holographs.

I think they are keen to claim the glory of capturing Solus and do not want to get sacrificed by the bloody politics of it all. To be honest, they are not wrong, we started with sixteen generals. As you can see, we are down to our last seven.

"We are so close to victory, my fellow sons of Devon" Basil pronounced as the unmoving Mandib Hussaris stood attentively in the War Room.

"We must attack Mount Amperia and finish the Xaracem filth, once and for all" Basil declared.

"I believe a Siege would be a better alternative!" Zeno intervened. Always the coward this one. That's why he has managed to survive for so long.

"A Siege is not glorious!" Basil retorted. On the other hand, I am shocked to see how Basil has survived at all. This hardheaded bastard has charged headlong into each battle since we started and has managed to come back unscathed every time.

"Glory is defined by the stories we tell, we can always tell them the Siege didn't weaken them enough, so we dropped in and killed them all!" Zeno reasoned.

"I mean we do have enough of that Xaracem meat to last us a few sols" Demetri jumped in with his rationale. Sols is what you humans call years; well, it depends on the star system. We follow Solus' revolution around its star as Sols, and that equals around 1.7 Earth years.

"Must not fail!" a thought reverberated through my mind. It was my brother's word when he spoke to me earlier.

"Glory, Siege or Rations, it does not matter. The most important thing is we need to finish this off as soon as possible. We have been here for 100 sols and are on the verge of reclaiming Solus," I interjected the bickering as I looked around. They were all looking up to me, including their own Hussaris.

"Our Overlords have spent Trimecans of Ment to fund this crusade of ours, they expect results within their lifetimes" I continued my reasoning.

"But your Overlord, the Nenoan King! is your twin, he is not dying anytime soon!" Zeno's cowardice resurfaced again.

"Nenoan Emperor!" I corrected him as my rear arms edged towards my blade. Zeno stepped back a little.

"Zios is right! We cannot delay this any further!" a holographic voice spoke. It was Theodora, the only matron General in our fleet. Trust me, when I say this, she really hates the term 'Second Sons'.

"What if it's a trap?" Demetri interjected. Zeno nodded his head fervently.

"Then we will die a glorious death in the name of Devon!" Basil butted back in.

"We have strategically cornered them into Amperia? How can it be a trap!" Theodora asked the council.

"We are the Second Sons we must proclaim new worlds as our domain! We cannot afford to –" Basil snapped back. The cacophony of their voices started giving me a headache. I stepped away and looked down at the infinite rows of Mandib Hussaris awaiting the decision of their Masters.

Out of my peripheral eye I saw a young Hussari twitching, the resolve within him, slowly dwindling as he saw his Overlords bicker like immature children. I saw myself in him. I was a Hussari once and my drunk General kept getting us in trouble with his hardheaded campaigns. I knew what that young Hussari felt in that moment. I wished the decisions of War were made in private, but it was Royal Decree of my brother, the Holy Devant Emperor Agamemnon, that all decisions be made with the Hussaris in attendance, they must know every hesitation and rationalization of their Overlords, as they make them. It somehow made them feel part of the decision. The Interstellar Warship Tigran, on which I stood bore the Royal Seal of Agamemnon, so I am not the one to argue with custom. This is why what I am about to do next is going to make my brother furious. I turned around.

"Generals!" I commanded. All of them looked at me with bewilderment.

"How about a vote?" I asked calmly. As I heard the seeds of doubt, germinate in the minds of the Hussaris. A vote is not rational, it doesn't give purpose to a war, it's just an arbitrary way of deciding based on personal opinions.

"Excellent idea! Sire!" Ruben jumped back in. He might think I didn't notice but I saw him smile in the corner when we started discussing the Siege. He will report this to my brother as soon as we are done with this Council. I hate that sycophantic bastard.

"All of you who are in favor of immediate attack on Mount Amperia, say aye!" I announced.

"Aye!" said Basil, without hesitation.

"Aye!" said Theodora, the General who joined holographically.

"Aye!" I said reluctantly. I didn't particularly like war, but prolonged war is decidedly much worse. I looked intently at Demetri hoping that he sees reason. But he didn't look up.

"Unless I don't know how to count, I believe we are settling in for a Siege!" Zeno declared pompously. Something flickered behind him as the membranes on my back stood up. I walked forward to examine it.

Theodora's Hologram was no longer there. Something was happening.

"Where is Theodora?" I asked Ruben.

"Must have left, discontent with the decision" Ruben said in his silk voice, which immediately did not make sense. Sure! she hated the Second Sons, but she was never a sore loser. She was one of our bravest warriors.

"Ruben ask the Engani to get me eyes on Sose!" I ordered Ruben to contact Bridge Control. The Devant Warship Sose was commanded by General Theodora, it was stationed just about Mount Amperia.

As I turned around to address the other Generals a deafening blast rocked our ship. I held onto the rails as the ship's artificial gravity turned off. Thousands of Hussaris were now suspended in the War Room.

* * *

The Saracen were a galactic alliance comprising of multiple alien species who had joined together to take over Solus some 10,000 Sols ago. They drove out the Mandib and claimed the birth planet of Devon for themselves.

After the initial exodus, the Mandib Civilization crumbled under poor leadership and guidance. We descended into chaos and darkness as the once great Devant Mandib were reduced to bands of bandits and scattered self-contained cults.

Sol after sol we rediscovered our religion as the fabled Three Kings emerged on Melchior, Gaspar and Nenos. The last one being my home planet. They trained Devant Missionaries and funded their pilgrimage to all the lost Mandib planets.

Through generations of hard work and toil they managed to build back their once lost civilization and decided to take back

Solus. They failed again and again as multiple fleets and missions were decisively defeated by the Saracen Occupiers.

Second Sons was an infamous alliance of bastards and spares who forged their own destinies away from the firstborns who inherited their father's throne. This was crucial for the rapid expansion of the Devant Mandib. Second Son's missions were expensive and were usually bankrolled by the aforementioned firstborns to expand their own domain by proxy. But those who failed usually became bandits and terrorized the trade routes.

My brother, the Holy Devant Emperor Agamemnon saw potential in the Second Sons as he commissioned a large fleet and redirected us to take back Solus. After 100 Sols of hard work, we are on the verge of greatness as we have cornered the Saracen and forced them to take refuge in the Hallowed Mount Amperia. But to our surprise and devastating failure of on-ground intelligence, the Saracen have now revealed their greatest weapon – The Starship Destroyer.

"The Destroyer has already claimed Warship Sose, Sire!" Ruben informed me as the Tigran moved away from the Mountain.

"They have forced our hand! We must descend to the surface and take out that Destroyer!" I declared to the Generals in the council as we regained gravity.

"But, the vote –" Zeno protested.

"If we settle in for a siege, they will take us out from the surface one by one!" I retorted.

"General Zios is right! We must attack right away!" Demetri said, calmly. I nodded in agreement.

"Move your Warships as far away from Mount Amperia as possible! Let's regroup after the maneuver" I commanded the Generals as the holographs turned off and Basil, Demetri and Zeno left the Nesset.

"Ruben! I need a headcount for all the Hussaris and Engani as soon as you can!" I commanded the Priest. He nodded and started to walk away. I grabbed him by my left rear arm.

"And do not waste your time on praying!" I warned him. He nodded a little more stiffly this time as he made his way out of the Nesset.

You might judge me unfairly for hating this pious Priest, but he is the only other Mandib, in this entire universe who knows of my telepathic connection with Agam.

Agam broke our promise to not tell anyone else of our special bond as he confided in his favorite priest. What was more insulting is how he appointed him as the Devant Solemn for Tigran and the Second Sons. To put it simply, I know a spy when I see one.

* * *

"We have a thousand Hussaris and a hundred Engani at our command, but —" Ruben reported. This was good news we started with much more, but we still have strong numbers left, plus the Engani can soften the defenses with their aerial attacks. I think we are in good position. Ruben looked distressed.

"But, what?" I asked him as he waited for my enquiry with bated breath.

"The blast from the Starship Destroyer — it hit –" the Devant Priest was stuttering. I raised my eyebrows to convey disappointment at his stuttering.

"It hit the Abattoir and the Ration Storage. We have lost all of our food!" Ruben continued in more clear terms.

"All of it?" I asked to confirm, to which Ruben nodded.

This was bad! We spent sols hunting down the Saracen to sustain us for this mission, and now we have lost all of it. A hungry army is never easy to command.

"I will talk to the fleet, see if we can procure some meat from them," I assured Ruben who nodded with a weak smile.

"A Siege is definitely out of question now!" I mumbled to myself.

"Did you say something, Sire?" Ruben interjected.

"Nothing! Is the Council ready?" I asked dismissing his question.

"They are, shall I summon the Hussaris to the War Room" Ruben asked with the same weak smile.

"Not this time!" I answered.

"But Sire! Our Hussaris have never fought this deep into the enemy territory, I think they deserve to know what their Generals are — " he groveled again as I moved past him.

"This is my ship! I will decide how things are done here!" I warned Ruben. Probably a bad idea as I will have to answer to my brother later. He nodded and gave way as I saw an expression of dread on his pale face. I could tell the blast from the destroyer has changed Ruben. He felt less cunning in his ways and more yielding to my command.

* * *

"I only want what is rightfully mine!" my Uncle Pittheus declared as I made my way onto his Warship Barbar, which was stationed above Nenos.

"Agamemnon and I, are the rightful heir to King Atreus, Nenos is ours!" I declared to my traitor Uncle and his Hussaris.

"Well, we can always extend this little civil war of ours to eliminate the number of rightful heirs!" my Uncle Pittheus spoke as he stroked his pet Riyalghri, an enormous saber-toothed reptile. It was turned over on his back, as my uncle scratched his underbelly.

"Our father funded your Second Son expeditions; it is the only reason you have your own domain now. You would be begging by the seminary if he hadn't done so" I snapped as the blood rose through my back.

"Ours! Ours! Ours! why can't you say 'mine'. It's like you and Agamemnon are joined at the hip" Pittheus mocked as his reptile let out a warning hiss. I backed away. Does he know about the connection between Agam and me. With all the advances in Mandib biology, telepathic communication is still considered odd and heretic.

"I know what it feels like to be loyal to my own blood!" I mocked back. The smile from Pittheus' scarred face vanished. He perched his rear arms above his throne and stood up to face me.

"You see this scar boy," he pointed towards his face.

"It's given to me by a Spikeback. A horned beast, the size of a Starship who is extremely territorial about his own domain" he turned around to let my imagination run wild. But all my mind could think was that Spikeback was not a very clever name. Why didn't he name it something grander if it is that humongous and deadly.

"Care to guess, where this territorial monster dwells?" he asked rhetorically.

"In my so-called domain, my planet, the one that I conquered all by myself while your father tossed a few Ments my way from his comfortable throne down there!" he pointed to Nenos.

"I am the Warrior, I was the one who expanded your grandfather's domain, and just because I was a born a few sols too late!

I will not be denied what I have rightfully earned" his green spit landed square in my face.

"Kill him! Now!" a voice echoed in my mind. I pulled my blade from behind me and handed it to my left front arm slowly.

The Riyalghri hissed as I plunged the blade into my uncle's heart.

His Hussaris charged at me with their blades, but I managed to take two of them out before subduing the third one.

"Your King is dead; you have no protection. I can give you refuge on Nenos!" I bargained with the Hussari Guards. They looked at each other with puzzled looks as they waited for more information. I released the one I subdued earlier to confirm my intentions.

One by one they dropped their blades and dropped to their knees and started praying in Devantian Chants. As I pulled the blade out of my uncle's heart his pet reptile charged at me. There was a sound of a deafening blast and then everything went dark.

* * *

"Are you sure you want to be in the Vanguard, my liege?" the Devant Priest Ruben pleaded as I stood in my quarters being outfitted with my Wingsuit.

"The immediate attack is my idea. It is only natural that I am the one who leads it!" I answered as the hunchback Outfitter fitted Dark Nenoan Armor to my back.

"But Sire you have only dealt with Xena-Saracen, during your raids on the outpost, I hear the deeper Saracen are bigger and stronger" Ruben continued his groveling.

"If I hadn't captured those outposts, we would still be sitting in the upper orbits with the Engani running meaningless raids on Saracen Cities!" I retorted as the hunchback motioned to retract my rear arms fully.

"I did not mean to diminish your contributions to the uh — Reconquest" he groveled some more. Seriously if Ruben hadn't been a Priest, he would make an excellent courtier.

"The Reconquest is almost complete, as soon as we take Mount Amperia and destroy whatever weapon they are hiding in its Caldera, we will become part of Devant history!" I sprinkled some religion to avoid his constant pestering.

"Will you join me in prayer before the descent, Sire?" he continued bickering.

"I am suited up, I am afraid I might not fit in the Devantry," I smiled.

"As you wish Sire! I will pray on your behalf" Ruben assured me with a weak smile.

I nodded in agreement with a weak smile. I just wanted him to leave me alone. He did eventually, after chatting with the Outfitter in the corner.

I walked towards the painting above the pantry in my quarters. It was my own artwork. I painted it when I was in the Seminary. It was a painting of Devon, as he walked on the floating bridge to bring the word of God to the Sitibi Tribe on Solus.

"Huh!" I let out a grunt as I realized how big of a religious nut I was in my youth. But as I thought deeper into my path to apostasy, I stopped myself. My thoughts were not my own, they were being watched by my brother Agamemnon. I only wish I had the same insight into my brother's mind.

"Guide me! Brother!" I thought to myself as I grabbed my Wingsuit Helmet and headed out of my quarters.

* * *

"Why did you shoot down Barbar while I was aboard?" I roared at my brother as the Courtiers left the Great Hall, with snooping reluctance.

"It wasn't me brother! I was with you when you killed that traitor Pittheus!" Agamemnon replied. As I looked deeper in his eyes. It was true, he commanded me telepathically as Pittheus was recounting his encounter with the Spikeback.

"I sense your confusion, but you must believe me when I tell you, the person responsible for shooting down the Warship Barbar was not me!" Agam reassured me again.

"Just get out of my head! You think I do not see your spying ways into my subconscious" I warned Agam.

"You asked me to stay with you. You said you felt alone! So I am always with you, guiding you, learning from you and above all looking after you" Agam placed his hand my shoulder. I shrugged it off.

"Do not patronize me! If it wasn't you then who was responsible for shooting the Warship down?" I corrected the course.

"It was Matheus!" he answered dejectedly.

"Cousin Matheus!" I asked to confirm. My brother nodded.

"He still sees the throne as a competition between you and me. And he chose to side with me, without my permission or knowledge. He thought he was doing me a favor," he continued with his explanation.

"But we grew up together! How can he –" I spoke as I looked at my brother.

"So did Uncle Pittheus and our father! But the Games of Thrones are unforgiving my brother and I would never let some title of King come between us. We were born at the same time; the throne is as much mine as it is yours!" he assured me but I stayed silent. The betrayal of Matheus stung me deep.

"In any case, I have scheduled Cousin Matheus' execution on the morrow" Agam interrupted the silence.

"What?" I exclaimed.

"I know you don't want him to die," he spoke as I felt his presence in my mind.

"But such are the rules of engagement, you try to kill a Nenoan Prince, then by Nenoan Law you must be executed for High Treason by Arachnocide.

A vivid image of my cousin Matheus' ribs being pulled out one by one and aligned alongside his four arms, flashed in my mind.

"I thought Pittheus would be the last of our family to die! I thought his death would end this needless civil war!" I protested as my brother walked away in his billowing robes.

"Only you and I can end this Civil War!" he spoke one last time before he exited the Great Hall.

The feeling of loneliness returned as I felt needles prick my brain from all sides.

* * *

"General! We are taking heavy fire from the turrets at the base of the mountain!" a voice roared on the holograph as I put on my helmet for the descent.

"Don't worry! I am coming!" I assured the Hussaris on the other side as I entered the drop chamber.

It was a round, transparent enclosure adorned with multiple life support systems and lined with heat shields inside and out. Its only purpose was to get me to the surface.

I entered the enclosure, as my wingsuit clicked into place. I looked at the deployment bay of Tigran one last time as I punched the flashing control panel and felt the floor beneath me drop. I was now descending into Solus, the birthplace of Devon and all of Mandib.

At first it was just blue skies, but it all turned to dark dust as I descended through the dark clouds.

"Engani! I need cover fire on those turrets, I am four away!" I instructed my air force to engage the turrets at the base of Mount Amperia.

"Understood General!" a voice echoed in my suit.

"3...2...1 Engage Wingsuit!" the voice inside the chamber rang as it opened to drop me just below the clouds. I was now falling on my own without the drop chamber.

I saw the ground as I jerked my rear arms to engage the wings. The heavy air rushed into my sides. The resistance decelerated my fall as I landed with a loud thud, behind the frontline forming a huge crater that made some of the soldiers move away in desperation. I looked up as I saw the Engani, fly by in their Silver Selterjets, only to circle back for another assault at the base of the Mountain.

As I climbed the small crater of my own making, a Hussari came rushing from the line and removed his visor.

"General! We must –" he started speaking as the roar of the Engani Selterjets drowned his voice. They swooped down towards the base and released ordinance just above the turrets. There was now a whole where the Saracen turrets were mounted before. The pestering Hussari who approached me was irrelevant to me as blood surged to my rear arms.

"Onwards!" I yelled as the Hussaris got up from their cover and charged the base of the mountain. I took flight, only to land in front of the charging Hussaris and lead them into the Mountain.

"Saracen!" a Hussari yelled on my right. I adjusted my visor to look through the dust created by the Engani Selterjet ordinance. There they were, pouring out of the hole, charging towards me, full gallop on their four legs.

I disengaged my wings as they retracted in the back and pulled my blades out with all four of my arms. The creature lunged at me as I drove the two blades on my front into his stomach and sliced him open. I sensed another coming at me from the side. I used my rear arms to drive my other two blades through him.

"Saracen filth!" I heard a Hussari yell in the distance as I saw him charge into a hoard of the attacking quadrupeds. He was immediately gored and split from all six of his limbs. It was horrible, but I had to focus on the Mountain. I saw the opening, a cave of sorts from where the Quadrupeds were emerging.

"Hussaris! Towards the cave!" I directed my army towards the cave, which was more a hole in the wall. I knew what was coming, as I saw hundreds being killed by the Quadrupeds before I reached the entrance.

"Basil! I need you to cover our retreat!" I yelled as I lopped off the head of the Quadruped Saracen that split one of the Hussaris in two.

"Understood General!" I heard rumbling at my feet. It was definitely Basil, he always likes to make an entrance. Blue Hussaris were descending to my right with a particularly adorned General Basil in the lead.

As we pushed through, what seemed like an infinite hoard. I saw another door open to our right. The Quadrupeds were now rushing through that door at Basil's army. The numbers emerging from the hole that we made dwindled as Basil lured them away with his larger army. I looked around to see my own Hussaris, but none were close. I decided to push through and get rid of the last trickle of Saracen Quadrupeds.

It was finally over; I was inside the mountain. As I looked around, I realized I was completely alone. I wiped blood off my visor to confirm. Yes! I was alone.

I took off my helmet, knowing that air of Solus is native to the Mandib, and I will probably be fine. The helmet clicked open as a warm feeling flooded me. I felt ecstatic.

"Am I hallucinating? Did they mix something in the air?" I tried to put my helmet on, but before I could find the adjuster, I heard a voice.

"Who are you?" the voice spoke softly.

* * *

"I will not face you in a duel!" I warned my brother as we walked in the Gardens of Albany.

"It is law, if a king dies without naming a successor, the first born is to take his place. But we were born at the same time, hence the law states we must duel until death or submission!" Agam explained to me.

"These Nenoan Laws have wiped out half our family, we need to rise above them!" I urged him again to find a better way.

"This law is Devant, not Nenoan!" he corrected me as we looked down at the waterfalls that descended into the dark abyss.

"I do not care!" I spoke as I tried to make out what is beyond the dark watery mist. Agam looked at me and then at the abyss.

"If I am to jump right now and die, you will be king by sunset!" he said nonchalantly.

"Stop being childish!" I warned him as I edged away from the waterfall hoping he would do the same.

"My point is, there is no easy way to do this, we have to fight in the duel or be a weak King forever?" he spoke as he turned around, his robe ends lightly drenched in water.

"Why a weak king?" I inquired.

"If you or I back out, proclaiming the other as King, the authority will always be in question. Any decision of one King, if deemed unpopular will be compared to how the other would have dealt with it. We must fight, for the good of Nenos!" Agam explained.

"What if I hurt you or maim you?" I asked looking back at the waterfall horizon.

"Then you will be maiming us," he spoke as he switched to telepathic communication.

"And as you very well know, you and I are the only one who can talk to each other this way, even if we are worlds apart!" he communicated with a warm smile.

* * *

"How are you able to talk to me — this way?" I asked the unknown voice in my head.

"Well we all talk this way!" the voice replied.

"All?" I thought to myself.

"Yes! All of us?" it read my thoughts.

"How can you read my thoughts?" I asked the voice as I silently remembered how Agam is the only one with this capability.

"It's very easy! I can show you!" the voice answered.

"Show me how?" I asked the voice as a blast went off in the distance. Basil and his Hussaris were still fighting the Quadrupeds outside.

"There is too much noise here. Climb up to the heart of the Mountain and I will meet you there!" the voice answered. Is this a trap? Am I hallucinating? Why does it feel so good here. It feels like —

"Home! and don't worry it's not a trap!" the voice spoke once again without prompt. I reluctantly moved forwards as I saw a small pathway that led upwards and curved away around a giant monolith.

After climbing for a while, the small pathway ran out. With my rear arms and the power of flight in my Wingsuit I managed to climb deeper into the Mountain. The curving caves and infinite caverns opened and then opened some more.

"Almost there! Just climb that ledge to your right!" the voice instructed me. I obeyed without hesitation. Basil and the rest of the fight felt like Sols ago. I grabbed a rock that protruded from the corner of the ledge, but it broke off as I engaged my rear arms to trigger the wingsuit. But as I braced for it to break my fall, I was suddenly suspended in mid-air. Something or rather someone had grabbed me.

A hand, much like mine pulled me up. What I saw next almost made me pass out. The being that had saved me from my fall just moments ago, stood before me, but what made me step back was the face that he was Mandib, just like me but a little bit different. I could not see an enclosure for his rear arms in his clothing. He turned around walked straight with his neck behind his back. His face looked exactly like mine, but somehow he felt different.

"I do not have four arms like you!" he replied in his actual voice. It was a sweet relaxing voice that almost reminded me of my father.

"King Atreus was a much gentler king than your brother!" he spoke again.

"Would you stop reading my thoughts!" I snapped.

"I am sorry! Force of habit! As you can see, we do not have secrets here in Mount Amperia" he apologized without looking back as we now walked into what looked like a huge cave, with one of its end overlooking the snowy expanse below.

"Welcome to Devon's Hollow!" he held out his hands which were the exact size of my forelimbs.

"So you are Devant too!" I interjected.

"God no!" he grimaced.

"I can read from your thoughts that you are an apostate, so if you would excuse me for my strong language but Devon can shove his entire religion up his dark abscess for all I care!" the mysterious stranger casually disrespected my religion. The punishment for which is exile or death in all Devant Worlds.

"Oh where are my manners? My name is Adar, you can call me Ada!" the stranger introduced himself.

"Have you been hiding here, from the Saracen!" I enquired as I looked around at his workshop. So many peculiar equipment of different shapes and sizes littered the shelves.

"I don't need to hide from Saracen, I am Saracen!" he declared. I pulled my blade in a flash. I knew the absence of his rear arms was suspect at best.

"No need to be violent! my dear descendant!" he continued to speak, unfazed by my blade.

"Descendant?" I stepped back.

"Yes! Descendant!" he confirmed.

"What? How?" I relaxed my blade.

"Ah! It's a long story, but let me make it short for you," he began as I sheathed my blade.

"You see, the Mandib never left Solus. The Devant Mandib were kicked out because they were too zealous. Capable of extreme violence as you yourself can attest!" Ada spoke as he walked around his lab checking readings on various gauges.

"The meat supplies," a chilling thought ran through my mind as I thought back to the tooth I found in breakfast.

"Don't worry! You are not a cannibal. But I should say, your methods of procuring supplies, is barbaric to say that least, I mean what kind of savage first conquers and then eats his enemy?" Ada taunted, as I felt his judgement wash over me. He was so different yet looked so much like me, well except for —

"The hands —" I thought to myself.

"Oh yeah! the hands, we used to have hands like you but we genetically selected ourselves out of that extra appendage. Those other hands are used for violence, we don't need violence in our highly developed secular galactic alliance." he read my mind again.

"Secular Galactic– what?" I asked confusedly, as I tried to walk like him, with my back straight. I failed as my rear arm bones crackled in defiance.

"Secular Galactic Alliance! When the Devants were gaining momentum, we were on the verge of unlocking the mysteries of the universe, we were already in contact with at least 18 different alien species, but thanks to Devon, everything went, completely wrong." he finished.

"What did Devon do?" I asked, defensively.

"Created a religion, intolerant of non-Mandib and outsiders!" Ada snapped back.

"So you kicked us out?" I asked, offensively.

"Well, you didn't leave without a fight? I can still see you haven't forgotten your violent ways!" he pointed towards my extended rear arms.

"Where are the others? The other Mandib I mean?" I asked as I retracted my rear arms.

"Immigrated to other Alliance Worlds! There is a war going on, if you missed it on your way in!" he resumed his gauge checks.

"You see! War causes immigration and to be really honest there isn't much left on this wretched planet for us to fight for." he declared as he made his way to the opening that overlooked the other side of the Mountain.

"Is that supposed to be one of yours?" he pointed at something, outside the opening. I rushed to his side to get a better look. No! No! No! There was a new Warship in the sky.

"It's the Nenoan Warship Atreus — it's my brother's vessel!" I spoke as words stuttered in my mouth. Turns out the opening was letting a lot of cold air inside.

"I will be right back!" Ada slipped away from my side, as I realized what he was about to do.

"The Starship Destroyer! Wait!" I called out as he turned back around.

"You are quite insightful, without your usual Mandib senses. How did you know I was about to engage the Helios!" Ada seemed intrigued.

"Instinct!" I mumbled as Ada looked at me for a more elaborate answer.

"The Starship Destro — I mean your Helios is stationed in the Caldera, atop Mount Amperia." I began.

"You are the highest lifeform I have seen in this Mountain, both literally and figuratively!" I continued.

"I mean somebody must have been operating it, might as well be you—" I spoke softly, realizing that he was just about to shoot my brother's ship out of the sky.

"You might not be a lost cause after all!" Ada wagged his finger at me and then rushed to his apparatus, which was now spewing dark smoke. He searched for something in the many chests that lined the walls of the cave. After much struggle, he stood still and closed his eyes.

After two blinks he walked to the far side and opened an ornate chest that was squished between two large boulders and pulled out a vial that contained something blue. It almost looked like blood, but as it moved in the vial, I realized it cannot be. He poured the vial, into the bubbling smoke and it vanished with immediate effect. A sweet smell filled the cave as I was reminded of the fragrant Gardens of Albany, where me and Agam used to walk and discuss the matters of government.

"Agam!" I turned back around to look at the descending Warship Atreus, a large part of which was now clearly visible to the naked eye.

"If he is here, he must know where I am, he knows what we are talking about, he can read me, just like you!" I panicked as I walked around his workshop. Ada simply smiled.

"Don't worry Zios, only I can read you. You probably disappeared from your brother's Hive, that's why he has come to personally rescue you!" Ada smiled some more.

"What is a Hive?" I asked as I looked at the descending ship outside.

"Well for your brother, it's more like a Comb, since he can only read you!" Ada muttered to himself. I looked at him with impatience as I waited for an answer to my original question.

"Well! Hive is a collective conscious that all of Mandib share!" Ada declared as he sat down to make a concoction.

"You mean all Mandib can read my thoughts?" I asked with a blank expression.

"Oh no no! my dear boy! Not every Mandib is built the same, some are more evolved. You are more evolved than all the Devant Mandib Filth, your brother is more evolved than you and I am the most evolved Mandib you have ever met!" he let out a chuckle as the steam from the concoction crowded his face.

"But how did he become more evolved? We were born the same —" I spoke with a choking sensation in my mouth.

"I do not know how he evolved, but it is impressive that he did it all on his own. But for you! I will help you, like I promised when you were at the base!" Ada spoke with fervent enthusiasm as if he was not about to be run over by the full force of the Second Sons and the Greatest Nenoan Warship — Atreus.

"Here! drink this, he poured the concoction in a cup and pushed it towards me!" I looked at the liquid inside the cup. It was dark and barely viscous; it moved every now and then to indicate that it is drinkable.

"This is what, you have been preparing ever since I entered your workshop," I wondered out loud.

"Actually I have been preparing it ever since you took off that god awful helmet of yours! But yeah drink up, it will bring you up the Mandib Evolutionary Chain!" Ada claimed. I had doubts but his presence in my mind assured me that what I was doing is correct.

I drank from the cup, as its watery residue spilled out of my nose. It felt like warm mud as it went down.

I heard a huge blast in the distance before I finally passed out.

* * *

"Princes Agamemnon and Zios will now engage in the Devant Succession Duel," the Grand Priest announced as Mandib from Nenos and other worlds gathered around the arena.

"Both Princes have forgone the right to choose a champion and will now fight for themselves." the Priest continued.

"That's more like it!" a spectator above my entrance punched the air.

"Princes! please step forward," the Priest declared. I stepped into the arena as I saw Agam emerge from the other side.

"Draw your blades!" the Priest commanded. I pulled my four blades as I saw Agam pull four parts of a spear from his holster and connect it into one.

"Do not relent brother! Give it your all!" Agam spoke telepathically as the duel bell rang. I lunged at my brother.

He ducked as I landed on the other side. He swiped his spear at my legs as I jumped to avoid it. I threw one of my blades which nicked Agam near the ear as it started bleeding blue.

He jumped and drove the spear straight in my direction, I moved just in time to pin his spear down with my leg as I ran my blade through his left arm. It gushed some more blood. I doubled down and ran my blade towards his other arm. My only intention was to hurt him enough, not kill him but he took this opportunity to break the spear in half and drive it into my lower leg. The pain was excruciating but I composed myself and stepped back, limping.

The anger in me bubbled up as I threw another blade at him, which he ducked proficiently but the throw was just the distraction as I ran my blade straight across his chest. Blue blood spattered across the white sands as he staggered back.

Something flashed as the image of the bloodthirsty crowd flickered. The next moment the spear ran through my stomach.

I blinked as the crowd changed again; I was surrounded by applause.

"Prince Agamemnon has chosen to spare the life of Prince Zios, Agamemnon Wins!" the Grand Priest declared. I breathed a sigh of relief as Agam hoisted his spear above his head.

"I shall now pronounce you King Agamemnon of Nenos as I —" the Grand Priest's word became blurry.

"You did good brother!" Agam's voice echoed in my head as I finally blacked out.

* * *

I woke up to see Ada leaning over me. I half expected him to let out an evil laugh for having captured me with the 'Evolved Mandib' ruse, but his smile never transformed into a laugh.

"Should be fine now! Try and read me, I will let you in!" Ada spoke calmly.

"What?" I spoke in blurred lines.

"We have to do this quickly your brother is almost here!" Ada spoke with urgency this time. I sat back up and looked at him.

Suddenly everything dissolved around me. One blink and I was looking at myself. Oh no wait, this is me from his perspective. I turned around and tried to make out what he thought of me.

"Uh uh uh! only vision, no thoughts! I don't want you to know my escape plan!" Ada blocked himself out.

"You have an escape plan?" I asked as I got on my feet.

"Of course I do! You didn't think I was going to martyr myself for the Saracen Cause!" he laughed. I just looked at him trying to penetrate his thoughts once more. But nothing.

"Stop trying to get in! I have something for you!" he walked to the other side of the workshop and pulled out a black slab. I heard another blast in the distance, this one was closer than before.

"This contains all of Mandib knowledge, old and new, inside and outside, Good and Devant. Do not let this fall into the wrong hands. I am only giving it to you because I see potential in your apostate ways!" he handed me the black slab as he started collecting his things and pushing them in a small sack. I looked at it from each angle there was no port or panel on this device. He bumped me on my head with what seemed like parchment.

"You get in to this the same way you get into my mind. Got it?" he asked as I nodded.

"Now for the escape plan? Are you ready?" he did some stretching as he started walking towards the exit.

"The entire Devant army is bearing upon the hole that I made, shouldn't you be going out the back?" I protested.

"Just follow me!" he said as we moved out of the cave. I pulled my blades ready to face my brother and be tried for high treason for colluding with the enemy.

But to my surprise nothing happened. Instead I saw something that was even more weird than the two handed Mandib living in the cave. All the Devant soldiers were frozen in place. General Basil was stuck with his Wingsuit about to take off, a manic smile upon his face. In the distance, a small ground ship, had landed, but the doors were still closed. We walked past the frozen Hussaris without any issues.

"See I told you I am more evolved!" he smiled as he walked past the frontline and into the barracks. I stopped in my tracks, as cold fear gripped my insides.

In the barracks was my brother standing in full Wingsuit Armor, but something was different about him. His eyes were moving.

"Ada! his eyes!" I turned around to pull Ada's attention towards my brother but he was gone, and suddenly everything started moving.

"Zios!" Agam's cold voice, that I once embraced as a warm feeling, creeped into my mind.

* * *

"So, you mean to say the Mountain is empty?" Agam inquired in the Nesset of Tigran.

"Yes, I cleared it myself!" I answered. I felt him peeping around my brain, but this time, I was able to hide behind a sort of veil. All my memories of Ada were hidden from Agam. In place of which I had conjured false memories of my lone conquest of Mount Amperia. His inquisitive eyes finally stopped.

"My brother! General Zios of Nenos has put an end to the Saracen " Agam turned towards the crowd of Hussaris and Generals gathered. Basil was giddy with joy, while Zeno cowered in the shadows.

"The Reconquest is complete!" he declared. A booming applause erupted across the entire War Room. As my brother looked towards the crowd I finally got a chance to look inside him. What I saw was — uh — something I never expected.

"I have another declaration to make!" Agam's voice echoed as the applause died down.

"As reward for my brother's brave deeds I give him our ancestral domain of Nenos, where he shall reign as King". Agam declared as I was bestowed with a meaningless gesture, the very thing I lost to him in a duel.

"And I will be Emperor" he thought to himself as I looked through his eyes at the crowds of Hussaris.

"And for me I will take the burdensome chore of rebuilding Solus and restoring it to its Pristine Devant glory!" the Hussaris celebrated once again, although the Tigran Hussaris who bore the seal of Nenos celebrated particularly loudly. All the Generals of the Second Sons who were either kneeling or leaning on something suddenly stood up in shock.

I turned my Mandib gaze towards them.

"We spent 100 Sols to recapture Solus; how can he just take it for himself?" Zeno thought.

"He brought his entire fleet here along with his Gigantic Warship, we cannot do anything to stop him —" Dmitri's thoughts unraveled slowly.

"Finally, I will be the only Emperor!" Agam's thoughts echoed in my mind. I get it now. The Hive! I can hear everyone all at once. My brother turned towards me and held out the hand to join him in celebration.

I got up and walked towards him as I conjured an inauthentic smile

* * *

I made my way down to the hangar after the celebrations stopped and snoring started across the halls. I had just a few items with myself, chief amongst them was the black slab that Ada gave me.

I walked to the end, where an Interstellar Lightship was parked.

"I shall call you The Nest!" I whispered to myself as I jumped into the ship and checked all the controls.

"Zios?" I heard a voice in my head. It was my brother Agam, outside the ship, in his night robes.

"What are you doing?" he asked concernedly as I stepped out of the ship.

"I am leaving!" I declared. I felt his gaze penetrate my mind for answers but this time I closed it off completely.

"Why? Where?" he feigned concern.

"Away from here, away from you!" I snapped back as I turned back towards the Lightship.

"What did you find inside the Mountain?" he asked, as his expression changed.

"The truth!" I replied as Agam's eyes widened.

"You cannot leave, you are the Devant Champion of Solus, the one who completed the Reconquest" Agam distracted from the topic. I moved closer to him.

"I know what you have done!" I spoke softly, his eyes searched for answers, once again he was unable to find them.

"STOP IT!" I roared as Agam pulled back from his efforts to infiltrate my mind.

"I know you were the one who ordered the shelling of Warship Babar, in an attempt to kill me, you failed but you did succeed in framing Cousin Matheus!" I recounted my brother's sins.

"I know you took over my mind and made me submit during the duel, so that you can pretend to spare me. You did it because you knew my rage will defeat you, if not my emotions" I continued as I walked forwards with my rear arm on the blade.

"What –" his mouth gaped open.

"I know, you murdered our father, because he saw the darkness in you and favored me as his successor!" I looked at him with rage, as my hand clasped my blade. He staggered back, tripping just a little on his overgrown robes.

"You killed millions in your lust for power! And I know you will kill many more going forward! I have decided to not be an instrument for all the destruction that is yet to come!" I slipped the blade back in my holster and turned around.

"But War! is the law of nature, if we don't compete for resources, we will be just a footnote on the pages of those history books you love so much!" Agam pleaded his case. I turned around. I pulled out my blade and lunged at him.

"So you want to write the whole book, by killing your father, getting rid of your family and maiming your brother! Is that how you want to win your precious wars?" I pushed the blade up against his neck as he let out a cackle.

"That's the Zios I know, the ruthless Devant Warrior!" he smiled as I pulled back my blade.

"I will eliminate the need for wars!" I declared as I entered my Lightship.

"How?" Agam asked over the starting roar of the engines.

"How?" he asked through our telepathic connection.

"How!!" he yelled, as his voice flooded my mind.

The ship took off and exited the Tigran. There was only one thing left to do.

Leave!

CHAPTER 2
MOTHERLAND

"**I** told you she was too sick to travel!" Meena scowled at her uncle as she held up her mother's hair while she hurled her breakfast into the hotel toilet.

"*Beta*! She called me every day ever since she got sick, to take her to Haridwar, how can I disregard her wishes, in this state, no less" Uncle Prateek explained from the other side of the rickety bathroom door.

"I am the Doctor! I know what she needs. Travelling should be the last thing she should be doing," Meena roared back as her mother hurled some more.

"These religious superstitions are the reason —" Meena continued before being interrupted by her mother.

"It's your airplane, I have only been on trains –" she scolded Meena as she went back down once more to expel what looked like discolored water.

"Train would have taken two days to reach this crowded eyesore of a city," she taunted as her mother kept her head down.

"Uncle! Did you call down to the reception for more water?" Meena asked from behind the door.

"Yes *beta*! It should be here soon," Uncle Prateek assured Meena.

A couple of minutes later, Meena and her mother Radha emerged from the bathroom of their hotel room, to find Uncle Prateek opening the door and signing for the water bottles.

"Well, I just got robbed!" he joked as he showed Meena the two ordinary water bottles and a bill slip that said 100 Rupees. Meena scoffed as she took one of the bottles from his hand and retreated back to her mother.

"Our mother wanted to go to Haridwar, before she died, but we weren't well enough, you know uh financially, to take her, Baba earned 75 Rupees in a day, how —" Radha started ranting with bated breath as a water bottle was thrust into her mouth by her daughter Meena.

"Mummy, will you stop? Grandma was never as sick as you!" Meena scolded her mother some more.

"Actually *beta* she was! Come to think of it she was your mother's age when she left us!" Uncle Prateek interrupted Meena.

"And you are telling me all of this NOW!" Meena bellowed.

"We didn't realize the coincidence but when Didi started speaking, I realized –" Uncle Prateek started explaining.

"Just shut it! I have had it with this family" Meena stopped her uncle. She looked for her purse and pulled out her phone.

"Yes! This is Dr. Sonkar speaking," Meena started her call.

"Get me Dr. Varshney! Yes I will wait –" Meena touched her mother's head to check her temperature. She felt the surging warmth as her heart sank some more.

"Hello! Dr. Sonkar, how are you? Have you reached Hari—" a voice came back on the phone.

"When was the last blood draw for Mrs. Sonkar?" she interrupted Dr. Varshney.

"Mrs. Sonkar?" Dr. Varshney inquired.

"Yes! My mother you fucking idiot!" Meena scolded the young doctor in training.

"Ah! Yes, let me check," there was a pause.

"Yes ma'am, two days ago, uh — Nurse Smriti drew the blood!" Dr. Varshney stuttered. Meena felt bad for calling him an idiot, after all he was just doing his job.

"There must be some left in the lab, check it for any genetic markers, any conditions that can be hereditary" Meena said, wiping the sweat from her eyebrows.

"Sure Mam! Let me write it down," he replied.

"How are they listed as a four-star hotel if they don't even have a working AC?" Meena taunted her uncle who now sat next to her sister, deep in hushed conversations.

"Did you say something ma'am?" Dr. Varshney inquired.

"No, you idiot, just do what I said. Run the blood for genetic markers and call me back when you are done!" Meena scolded her young protégé. She felt bad, again. The heat was getting to her.

"But ma'am, there can be thousands of conditions, do we have any symptoms to narrow it all down?" Varshney asked. Meena put her hand on the phone mic and turned towards her mother and uncle.

"Grandma! Did she have any other symptoms, which Mummy does not have!" Meena asked her uncle and looked at her mother. He threw his hands in the air and looked at his sister, moving restlessly against the hard pillow of the hotel bed.

"*Beta*! I don't really know, I was young, they usually kept her away from everyone, once she got sick. Your mother was the oldest –" Uncle Prateek groveled as he stopped to look at his sister. Meena felt helpless.

"Wait!" he interrupted Meena as she turned back to order Dr. Varshney to run panels for symptoms related to low blood pressure and arrythmia, the symptoms that her mother already had.

"Amma's eyes were a different color towards the end!" Uncle Prateek exclaimed.

"What color?" Meena stopped to inquire.

"Umm –" he mumbled.

"Were they yellow?" Meena prompted.

"Yes! Deep yellow!" Uncle Prateek confirmed.

"Check for Wilson's and Crigler-Najjar and report back to me!" Meena instructed Dr. Varshney as she hung up the phone to check her mother's eyes.

They were clear.

"No copper ring around the iris so it's definitely not Wilson's" Meena mumbled under her breath.

* * *

Haridwar was a bustling pilgrim city nestled in the valleys of the lower Himalayas. It was home to more than 2 million people, and it clearly showed with the slow-moving traffic across its narrow roads, built into the side of the mountains. On one such road, that led to a holy riverfront called Vishnu Ghat, a small cab swerved around bikes and cycle rickshaws. In this cab rode the Sonkar family on their way to honor the wishes of the ailing Radha Sonkar, with her daughter Dr. Meena Sonkar, sitting by her side in the back of the cab and her younger brother and Meena's Uncle Prateek Kurmi riding shotgun with the colorful driver who pointed out every little temple that seemed to sprout up on all the little organic squares of the old city.

"Why aren't you going to Har ki Pauri, it is the best ghat for pilgrimage" the cab driver pointed out as they passed a bridge.

"Our grandmother came to Haridwar, when she was sick. She visited Vishnu Ghat and immediately felt better, so we are taking my sister there as well." Uncle Prateek answered the driver's question.

"Great! Grandma was sick too?" Meena exclaimed in the back as she held her mother's hand.

"We don't really know, Baba told us –" Uncle Prateek began his apology.

"Seriously! Where were you when we were taking family history!" Meena interrupted her uncle. Her mother squeezed her hand to make her stop.

"We are here!" Uncle Prateek announced as he opened the door and jumped out of the car.

They walked down to the ghat as both of them helped Radha down the riverfront steps. She was incredibly weak and was coughing incessantly.

"She needs to take a bath in the holy water of Ganga" Uncle Prateek announced.

"You need to help her!" he signaled Meena towards a small chain enclosure where a couple of fully clothed women were taking dips into the river.

"I am not going to be a part of this madness! I have been really patient about her visiting a city so far away from home, I even came with you to make sure she is okay, but I cannot help her take dips into that bacteria ridden water, while she has a fever!" Meena walked away in protest as tears welled up in her eyes.

"*Beta*! I cannot take her to the women's area" Uncle Prateek called out as Meena walked up the crowded steps and towards the parking lot. Tears ran down the side of her nose as she recounted the last few months.

The bathroom fall was just the start as her mother's health deteriorated faster than anything she has ever seen in her short medical career. The worst part was that no amount of specialists could figure out what was wrong with her. She herself contacted everyone from her college professors to renowned diagnosticians across the world. All of them said one thing.

"Her organs are failing but we do not know why!" a general statement echoed in her mind.

All she could do was treat the symptoms but unless she could figure out what's actually wrong with her, she was only prolonging the inevitable.

"Madam! Madam! Can you spare some money for food, I haven't eaten in a week," a boy's voice pulled Meena back to reality. Feigning weakness, the sweet beggar boy repeated his request. Meena wiped her tears and looked for some loose change in her purse, all she could find was a 50 Rupee bill.

"Here! And you would be dead if you didn't eat for a week!" she smiled through the tears as she handed the little boy the money and tussled his hair.

"Which province are you from Madam?" a voice came from her left. She turned to face it. It was another boy, a little older, maybe in his 20s, but with a full-on Saffron Brahmin garb and a small table with a lot of books stacked on top of each other.

"Excuse me!" Meena asked, even though she clearly heard the question the first time.

"I asked which state are you from?" the Brahmin Priest asked calmly.

"I am from the South! See, I don't need any —" Meena tried dismissing the young solicitor. She did not believe in the superstitions that dangerously plagued her mother and uncle.

"And were you born in the South?" the Priest asked, with a smile on his face.

"No, I was born in the Central Province?" Meena answered without a thought.

"Central Province! Central Prov – here it is?" the Priest sifted through multiple volumes of folded parchment at his feet and pulled up one marked "Central Province" in the most atrocious writing she had ever seen.

"Can you tell me your parent's name and where are they from?" the Priest asked in a curious voice as he unfurled the long parchments held together by poor binding and brown tape. Meena stepped closer to inspect.

"Arvind and Radha Sonkar," Meena said hesitantly, unable to explain the magnetic charm of the Young Priest. He looked through multiple rows, while looking up at Meena multiple times.

"Sonkars from Indore?" he enquired.

"No we are from Bhopal!" she answered as the Priest dived again into the parchment.

"No Sonkar in the last 50 years from Bhopal" he answered as she realized what she was looking at. Her eyes widened and she looked around for her uncle. The crowd moved in erratic patterns as she tried to spot her uncle. Dejected, she turned her hopes towards the old parchments. An unknown flicker of hope, rekindled inside of her.

She had read about this or maybe heard it somewhere in passing but what she was looking at were the Lineage Records that went back hundreds of years. The young Priest who deciphered the records, was from the fabled Pandas Sect who kept accurate historical records for almost every family that visited this holy site.

"Can you check, for Kurmi, from Sagar" she leaned in. She knew that her grandmother visited this ghat some years ago and she belonged to a small city in Central Province called Sagar.

The Priest reopened the parchments and started going through the names. The writing was horrible, but she tried to keep up with the young Priest who was reading the Parchments at breakneck speeds. By comparison, her own writing as a doctor now seemed like exquisite calligraphy.

"Mewalal and Sudha Kurmi from Sagar!" he exclaimed as Meena leaned in further to confirm. She did remember her grandmother's home was called Sudha Sadan (humble abode), so this might just be her.

"Yes! Yes!" she prompted as her heart raced faster and faster. She was not sure what she was looking for, but these crumbling volumes were essentially just sparsely detailed family histories.

"Yes she visited here in 1976," the Young Priest continued. She recounted her mother telling her that her own grandma died when she was just two. The timeline does line up since Meena's mother was born in 1975.

"I have records for three centuries in this vein!" the young Priest exclaimed.

"What do you mean by 'vein'?" Meena asked as a passerby bumped into her shoulder.

"I can trace your lineage for 300 years! Look!" the Priest pointed at the parchment as he rotated it towards Meena. She looked at it intently, he was right. She could see her maternal lineage all the way back to 1700s.

"Sudha Kurmi - 1975 - 48, Uma Devi - 1968 - 49, Shakuntala Devi - 1939 - 51, Phoolbai - 1909 - 47..." Meena traced her maternal lineage as she muttered the names under her breath. Some quick math told her that all these women visited Haridwar when they were around 50, just like her mother. Her heart sank as she kept reading the names and the pattern kept repeating. Maybe they were all sick just like her, her heart sank lower.

"Padma Bai - 1863 - 57, Bhavani Devi - 1863 - 73... What the hell?" Meena mumbled to herself.

"What does this mean how can two of my grandmothers visit at the same time?" she showed the text to the young Priest. He looked at it intently.

"Ah! Because they visited together! The daughter Padma Bai was 57 and the mother Bhavani Devi was 73" the Priest explained. This was shocking news. The pattern of early death followed for 175 years and suddenly there was Bhavani Devi who visited when she was 73. Meena's head spun as she processed this information. She pulled out a water bottle and drank from it as she continued reading.

"Bhavani Devi - 1829 - 23, Uma Devi - 1829 - 47, Janaki Devi - 1829 - 67, Sundari Bai - 1829 - 85, Amba Devi - 1829 - 105." Meena's jaw dropped as she read the record of this visit in 1829.

Five generations of her grandmother visited Haridwar together in 1829, the eldest of them was 105 years old.

What was more surprising was what came next as Meena continued to read.

"Rewabai - 1806 - 105 ... Damini Devi - 1799 - 110 ... Kaveri Devi - 1799 - 102 ... Tarabai - 1787 - 154".

"Her great grandmother Tarabai was 154 years old when she visited Haridwar!" the thought rang through her mind as she stepped back from the parchments which curved at the seams, aching to roll back to their original scroll form.

* * *

"They used to eat well, back in the day!" Uncle Prateek explained as their cab sped towards the airport.

"A 154-year-old woman cannot make it to Haridwar, do you even realize how hard it was to make this journey, back in the day?" Meena fought back from the backseat as her mother slept on her shoulders.

"It is false hope! We must not talk about this in front of your mother," Uncle Prateek warned.

"But if there is a cure, for her disease. We must try!" Meena protested as her mother woke up asking for water. Meena grabbed the bottle from her bag and carefully held it to her face.

"We don't even know where this 154-year-old Tara Devi lived?" he said hesitantly.

"She lived in the Central Provinces in a village called Patauna!" Meena answered as she remembered the atrocious handwriting of the Young Priest's ancestor.

"I urge you to let her live her last days in peace!" Uncle Prateek turned around.

"Is this supposed to be peaceful?" Meena pointed to her wheezing mother, who let out infrequent coughs. The driver honked and yelled abuses out the window to a rickshaw driver who now stood diagonally blocking the way.

Meena looked at her watch.

* * *

"The Pilgrimage was a bad idea! Her O2 sats are below 90 and Platelet count is way down!" Dr. Khan reported as he talked to Meena outside her mother's private room. She hung her head in shame.

Dr. Ahmed Khan was Meena's mentor at the Gandhi Medical College and Teaching Hospital in Chennai. He was also the lead attending on her mother's case. He worked tirelessly running every test to figure out what could be wrong with her but there was no explanation.

"And the genetic tests you ordered, they all came back negative!" Dr. Khan reported further. Meena wanted to discuss the unusually long age of her great-great Grandmother, but she knew better to challenge Dr. Khan with unverified facts. For all she knew those parchments could have been forged to scam more money out of innocent tourists.

"Um... Doctor, what can be the possible reasons someone can live to be over 100?" she rephrased the questions to avoid the personal angle.

"Can be many things," he mumbled as he sifted through the blood culture reports.

"Like?" Meena prompted as Dr. Khan looked at her curiously.

"Good genetics, better environment but the most consistent answer is diet. You must eat the right things for your whole life if you want to cross that age!" he answered with a puzzled look.

"Can it be genetic?" she asked with a smile.

"It can be. The blue zones in the world usually consist of a bunch of families, yet they still give all the credit to their simple diet!" he suffixed the answer.

"Diet! Diet! Maybe Uncle Prateek was right!" Meena thought to herself as she turned towards Dr. Khan yet again.

"I would like to use my PTO?" she asked Dr. Khan.

"Really! I mean you just came back and I need you —" Dr. Khan stopped short as he looked at the resolute expression on Meena's face.

"Okay how much do you want?" he asked hoping the answer would be something short.

"As much as you can give me!" she answered.

* * *

"*Beta*! This is madness, she needs you by her side," Uncle Prateek protested as Meena put her luggage in the back of the cab.

"I am doing this for her! I need to find out how Amba Devi avoided this mysterious illness" Meena explained as she went inside the house to fetch some more stuff.

"*Beta*! What if you can't find anything and we lose your mother, before you are back?" Uncle Prateek asked, but he soon knew he had made a huge mistake as Meena turned around with fury in her eyes. He looked at her with love as she broke down.

"I don't know what to do?" Meena bawled, as she dropped to the ground.

"I cannot see her suffer anymore!" she cried as the cab honked outside.

"Give us 5 minutes!" Uncle Prateek urged the driver.

"*Beta*! These are forces beyond your control. You tried your best, but you need to say your goodbyes!" he hugged her as she cried in her arms.

"No!" she pulled herself away from him.

"I will not sit by and do nothing!" she roared and at that moment Uncle Prateek knew he could not stop her.

"Just call me when you get there! OK?" he hugged her once again. She nodded against his chest.

"I will take good care of your mother!" he assured her, to which she let out another sob and a short snort.

* * *

"Madam! Madam! Patauna is here!" the bus conductor woke up Meena as she cleared the drool off her face.

She picked up her purse and made her way to the front of the rattling bus. It smelled of diesel and Meena was sure she tasted metal when she woke up. She stepped out, as a little boy lowered her luggage from the top of the bus.

"Which way to Patauna?" she asked the conductor.

"Just follow this small road, for 10 minutes and you will be there!" the conductor answered as he looked up and down at this city girl in her tight Jeans and Kurti.

It was true. Meena was completely out of her element. She was born in a city and grew up in an even bigger city as his father moved around for his government job. She never experienced anything remotely rural. Despite all of this she was not afraid. She actually felt relaxed, and actually more home than she ever felt anywhere else.

"This is definitely the place!" she mumbled to herself as her lungs pulled in fresh air and the wind untangled her hair. She picked up her luggage and started walking.

There were multiple motorbikes that passed by her as she walked slowly and carefully, before someone finally stopped to enquire what a city girl is doing in a village.

"Where are you from?" a man in his 20s stopped his scooter and asked Meena.

"I am from Chennai; I am looking for –" she tried to explain her purpose but stopped. She did not know the surname of Tara Devi. She was just mentioned as Tara Devi - 1787 - 154. She racked her brain to come up with the latest ancestors, she could think of that was also from Patauna.

"Bhavani Devi's house!" she completed her sentence, cursing herself. Bhavani Devi visited Haridwar in 1863 with her daughter.

"There is no Bhavani Devi, in this village!" the young man spoke, quite rudely. Meena realized how over-protective, the rural people are. She tried to think more.

"Is there someone older, in the village I could talk to?" she enquired as a smile appeared on the young man's face.

"You can talk to Uncle Kanchan, he is the oldest we have?" he joked as he shifted forward on the bike. Meena had a choice to make. Either sit on this complete stranger's bike and trust him to take her to this Uncle Kanchan or refuse his offer and wander aimlessly in this unknown place.

"I –uh–" Meena stuttered. The man smiled again.

"My name is Abhijeet Verma, I am the Sarpanch (head) of Patauna?" he pointed to a poster at the front of his bike. It had couple of people standing to the right and to the left was the man on the bike. His hands were folded in greeting with a small hill as his election sign. The top of the poorly glued pamphlet read — Award your precious vote to Son of Patauna – Shri Abhijeet Verma.

Meena looked back at the man as he smiled graciously. Somehow him being a politician was worse than him being a stranger, but her rational mind soon took over and she realized that not every politician lives a life of crime. She nodded as the man grabbed her suitcase and put it between his legs on the scooter. She sat on the back, with her legs on one side and they set off.

"Is this electric?" she asked, for the scooter did not make any sound as it sped forward.

"Yes! I bought it last year, helps with the farming. Petrol is just too damn expensive nowadays!" he joked as Meena relaxed a bit more.

"Where are you from Madam?" he asked graciously.

"I am from Chennai," Meena answered.

"But you don't look like you are from the South!" he immediately interrupted her.

"And you don't look like a Sarpanch!" Meena snapped back. He was too young to be a village head. He laughed.

"My family is from around here! We moved to Chennai because of my father's job." she answered.

"Ahh! Welcome back home, then!" he let out a smile as she looked at him in the rearview mirror.

* * *

"Bhavani Devi! No, I don't know about that?" the old man spoke in his broken language, which Meena didn't understand much, but she got the point.

"I am sorry!" the village head Abhijeet apologized. Meena's heart sank as she realized, her journey had finally failed. Maybe if she hurries back, she can still spend some time with her mother.

"NO!" a voice inside her corrected her defeatist attitude.

"Amba Devi?" she asked old man Kanchan, if he knew the 105-year-old grandmother who visited Haridwar in 1829.

"No! I don't know Anja Devi!" the old man refuted with annoyance.

"Not Anja, baba Amba!" Abhijeet corrected him.

"No! No! I don't know Amba!" the old man replied, his irritation now amplified.

Kanchan Choudhary was almost 96 years old and had lived in Patauna for almost all his life. Well except for a brief stint in the Indian Military. He was blind in one eye and sat under the Neem Tree for the better part of the day. His family, which comprised of over 28 people, asked him to come inside all day but his response every time was, — 'It's too hot inside!'.

"Thank you Baba!" Meena thanked the old man as she put her hand on his wrist. He turned his head towards her and looked at her fully for the first time.

"Sita!" he mumbled.

"My name is Meena!" she replied.

"Where have you been?" he asked misty eyed.

"I am —" Meena tried to correct him again but she stopped. Maybe her touch reminds him of someone. Someone who she might be related to.

"We used to meet every day near the hillock, why did you stop?" old man Kanchan spoke with a quiver in his voice.

"Which hillock?" Meena asked, hoping that this might be where her maternal ancestors lived. Kanchan jerked his hand away from her and suddenly realized he was hallucinating.

"Which hillock? Baba?" Meena pursued the old man as he started walking back towards his house. She started following him as a woman in the house helped Kanchan up the stairs and into the front room. Meena looked at the house in disbelief. It was a poorly constructed house, with blue paint and exposed brickwork on the left side. She was so close.

"There is only one hillock around here!" Abhijeet spoke with a smug smile. Meena turned around and looked at him with hope.

"I can take you there if you want?" he offered. Meena smiled.

* * *

That night in her room at the small Townhouse Hotel, Meena searched and searched for any references to the Black Hillock or Kali Pahadi as Abhijeet described it. Her little laptop was running out of juice, as a routine blackout forced her to turn on her phone flashlight and drop the brightness on her laptop to save some more battery.

At last she found it, it was not much but it was the two words that made it jump out — 'The Witches of Kali Pahadi' a letter, addressed back to his home in Manchester by a British Officer who fought in the Anglo-Sikh Wars of the mid-19th Century.

'Doctrine of Lapse' the British called it when they took over the princely states of the Central Provinces, which had no male heir. After quelling multiple rebellions lead by female claimants to the thrones, the British came across a curious place, one that scared some and fascinating others.

The Kali Pahadi or the Black Hillock, which was a small hill across the Tarbhanga River that flowed alongside Patauna, stood out on the relatively plain surrounding. The hillock's only residents were a group of old women, who infrequently married their daughters into the nearby villages, to produce heirs, who upon maturing returned back to the Hillock.

Under the Doctrine of Lapse, the Hillock was to be the property of the British Raj, since it was passed generation by generation to female heirs. But when they tried to enforce this policy, they got an unnatural pushback from the surrounding villages who considered the old matrons as spiritual beings.

The British spent years to dispel this Cowen of Witches occupying a small part of their domain, through various means that ranged from policy to brute force, but time after time they failed until one particular morning in the May of 1864, they found the hillock abandoned and their maternal residents, visibly missing. The British sent Godwin May and his platoon to inspect, who found nothing but some abandoned huts and a small spring pond that turned dark as they approached it.

"This is it!" Meena thought to herself as she closed the laptop and stepped out of her room, into the cold night.

There was no moon in the sky, but still there was no darkness. Unlike the city, the stars were brighter and more beautiful than she had ever seen. These were the same skies her grandmothers saw as they settled in for the night, in their little hill community. A feeling of pride welled up inside her as she appreciated the night sky, littered with twinkling lights. A smile appeared on her face as she realized that the routine blackout was somehow the best thing to happen tonight.

For a moment she forgot about the pain of her mother's illness that had plagued her for the last few months and basked in the anticipation of finding her long lost Motherland.

* * *

As the sun rose a new hope took home in Meena's heart while she sat on the small scooter behind Abhijeet. What if there were people living there already. Maybe they were her Centurion Ancestors and could tell her how to save her mother.

"I cannot go with you to the Hill!" Abhijeet slowed down the scooter.

"Why?" Meena asked.

"Well –uh –" Abhijeet hesitated.

"What?" Meena pushed back.

"Well because it's haunted!" Abhijeet blurted out.

"What do you mean it's 'haunted'? Meena asked.

"Anyone who goes near the hillock hears voices and is eventually driven mad," Abhijeet said.

"So you are afraid you will go mad!" Meena interrupted him with a smile, that he saw in the rearview mirror.

"No it's just! –uh– I have heard stories of Witches who live on the Black Hillock!" Abhijeet said as the ride got more tough. The smooth road had finally run out and now they were trudging through poorly paved red soil.

"What kind of stories? Tell me some!" Meena asked, hungry for some local perspective after reading Godwin's Letter.

"You just heard it!" he answered.

"There was a man who fell in love with a Witch from the Black Hillock, and after she dispossessed him, he was never the same!" Abhijeet spoke in a low voice. A bump on the road readjusted Meena's spine some more. She hated sitting with her legs to the side.

"Who told you this story?" Meena asked as she squeezed Abhijeet's shoulder for some support.

"My mother! I thought she was trying to scare me to sleep, but I now realize that the story was true!" Abhijeet spoke with a tremor in his voice.

"Who was the man who fell in love with the Witch?" Meena asked.

"You just met him!" he answered.

"Old man Kanchan?" Meena asked. Abhijeet nodded as the small hillock with black rocks at the top and lush green vegetation at the bottom hove into view.

* * *

Meena waved goodbye to Abhijeet as she walked towards the Black Hillock with her small backpack. He waved back, but he did not leave. As she walked on the dry ground with odd weeds here and there, she saw small pieces of animal carcasses. Her heart sank. Maybe there was something sinister about this place.

It was called the Black Hillock after all. But as she took more and more steps her walk turned into a stride.

"Meeeena!" she heard Abhijeet call out, as he saw that the girl from the city that he had just dropped near the haunted Hillock was now running towards it.

But she was not possessed, instead she felt ecstatic. She felt free. A smile appeared on her face as she reached the small path that led up the hill. To her surprise it was lined with small huts with pretty little courtyards in the front.

She was right. There were people living here. She had finally found it. As she approached the first hut at the base of the Hill an old woman emerged slowly from it.

"Namaste!" Meena greeted her with the biggest smile, hoping she would talk back.

She didn't. She just pointed up. Meena's smile vanished. Were they not happy to see her? Was she not one of their own? Thoughts raced through her minds as she snapped back to reality.

"Do you want me to go up?" Meena asked. She smiled and nodded. Her own Mother's smiling face flashed in her mind.

Meena obeyed her and walked on the small road, paved by the footsteps of the residents in the Black Hillock. Every hut she ran into had a lady in it. Some were old, some were less old, but none were young. This was a good sign.

As Meena approached the top of the hill, she felt as fresh as when she started at the bottom. She slowed her walk.

"Am I hallucinating? Why am I not tired?" Meena wondered to herself considering she travelled for two days to reach Patauna, had barely slept last night and now felt more relaxed unlike anything before.

She looked down from the top, to see if she could spot Abhijeet. He wasn't there. Her heart sank with disappointment. He was starting to grow on her. She kind of liked him too, deep down. His rustic charm and accented banter was something that she felt attracted to. Well at least she did, before he abandoned her just now. She compartmentalized the anger she felt and kept walking as she came up on a small spring that turned into a waterfall that fell to the other side of the hill.

"This must be the black pond that Godwin was talking about!" she thought to herself as she approached the spring pond that didn't look dark at all. It looked completely transparent as she saw small silver fishes swim at the bottom. They were so reflective that she would not have known of their presence if they hadn't moved from side to side.

A woman emerged from the opposite side of the small path that Meena had traversed. She had a walking stick in her hand as she looked at Meena. A smile appeared on her face as she walked to the opposite side of the spring.

The old woman started gesturing at something when Meena realized that it was the same old woman that welcomed her at the base of the hill.

"How could she have climbed the hill so fast, at her age?" Meena thought to herself as the lady kept pointing at the pond.

"Do you want me to drink the water?" Meena asked. The woman nodded.

"But it might have —" Meena protested before the woman dropped the walking stick and bent down to the level of the spring pond.

She made a cup with her hands and dipped it into the clear water. As the water rushed into her hands she looked up and smiled at Meena once more, before pulling her hands up as she drank the water.

"Well if it is good enough for an old lady, it's good enough for me!" Meena smiled some more and bent down to get a drink.

The water was cold. Colder than anything she has ever tasted, yet it didn't hurt as it went down. It satisfied a thirst that Meena didn't even know she had.

"It's good! Really good!" Meena complimented the water as she looked up. The old lady was gone. She turned around to look for her, but the small path she walked on was also gone. It was covered in the same weeds that she encountered on her approach to the hill. She turned back to look at the pond. It was still transparent, but the fish were visibly missing.

In the place of the old lady stood a small guava tree with low hanging fruits the size of tennis balls. She put down her backpack and pulled out her water bottle. She emptied it in the nearby bush and dunked it into the spring. It bubbled for some time and then it was finally full.

She closed the bottle and put it back in the bag. She walked around the pond towards the Guava Tree as she pulled some fruits down and carefully stored them in her bag.

"Meeeeeena!" she heard a distant voice. She turned around to look where the voice was coming from.

It was Abhijeet, he was still there, waiting for him at the bottom.

* * *

The car stopped in front of the Gandhi Medical College and Teaching Hospital in Chennai. Meena shot out of the car like a bullet and ran towards the private wards. She knocked over a couple of people on her way as she approached her mother's room.

"Mummy!" she burst into the room with manic energy. But she wasn't there. Instead there was a large man, who put down his pudding cup on his large belly as he turned away from the TV to look at his intruder.

"Who are you?" the large man asked as he sat up in his mother's bed. Her heart sank as she dived for the file on the counter near the door.

"Manoj Agarwal, Heartburn and Fatty Liver" she read the file. They must have moved her. But where? Is she already —

"NO!" her inside voice snapped again as she exited the room and ran towards reception, before colliding headfirst into Dr. Khan.

"Dr. Meena! You are back!" Dr. Khan exclaimed as he recollected his patient files, that had spilled onto the floor.

"Where is my mother?" Meena asked with a knot in her throat.

"Well your Uncle! He requested we discharge her since she wasn't recovering —" Dr. Khan's statement was cut short as Meena broke into another run.

A tear-filled taxi ride later, she arrived home as she knocked on the door with all her strength. Uncle Prateek opened the door as he looked outside to see if someone was with her.

"*Beta*! Why didn't you call?" Uncle Prateek asked in a low voice.

"Where's Mummy?" Meena asked, wiping her tears away.

"She's uh –" Uncle Prateek looked at her with concern.

"WHERE IS SHE?" Meena roared.

"She is in the bedroom, sleeping!" he answered. Meena ran past him and burst into the room. Her mother looked even more weak now. Her cheeks were sunken and the dark circles beneath her eyes were bigger than ever.

Meena slung the backpack around to the front and pulled out the water bottle and the Guava fruits that she picked from the Black Hillock.

"What are you doing, *beta*?" Uncle Prateek protested, with some concern, but Meena wasn't listening.

"Mummy! Wake up!" she whispered in her mother's ear. She opened her eyes at once and looked at her with the same love she had shown for all her years growing up. She was glad to see her daughter one last time.

"Drink this!" she brought the water bottle to her face. She titled her neck to take a sip and let out a cough.

"You need to get her up – wait let me help!" Uncle Prateek sprang into action, still clueless to Meena's Plan. But before they hoisted her up she signaled for some more spring water with her thin fingers.

Meena smiled as tears formed in her eyes and put the bottle on her mother's lips again. She drank as much as she could before she grabbed Meena's wrist. Meena pulled away and laid down her mother on the bed.

"What now?" Uncle Prateek asked.

"Now we wait!" Meena said, with the same teary smile. As she held her wrist where her mother just gripped. She could still see the imprints of her fingers.

* * *

The next morning Meena woke up near the bedside of her mother as a hand prodded her to wake up.

"Meenu!" a voice called out. Meena turned over, she was very tired from her trip.

"Meenu!" the voice called again. Meena felt irritated before realizing that only one person in the world called her 'Meenu'. She sprang up to find her mother looking intently at her.

"I am hungry!" she said as Meena's blurry eyes met her mother's face. Uncle Prateek burst into the room. He always slept lightly, more so since his sister got sick. He found Meena rummaging through her backpack and her sister sitting up in the bed smiling.

"Eat this!" Meena offered the Guava fruits to her mother. She took a bite and then another until she finished the whole thing.

"That! — was delicious!" she said with fleeting strength. Meena offered her another.

"What does this mean?" Uncle Prateek asked Meena.

"It means that — we are moving to Patauna!" Meena answered with a big smile.

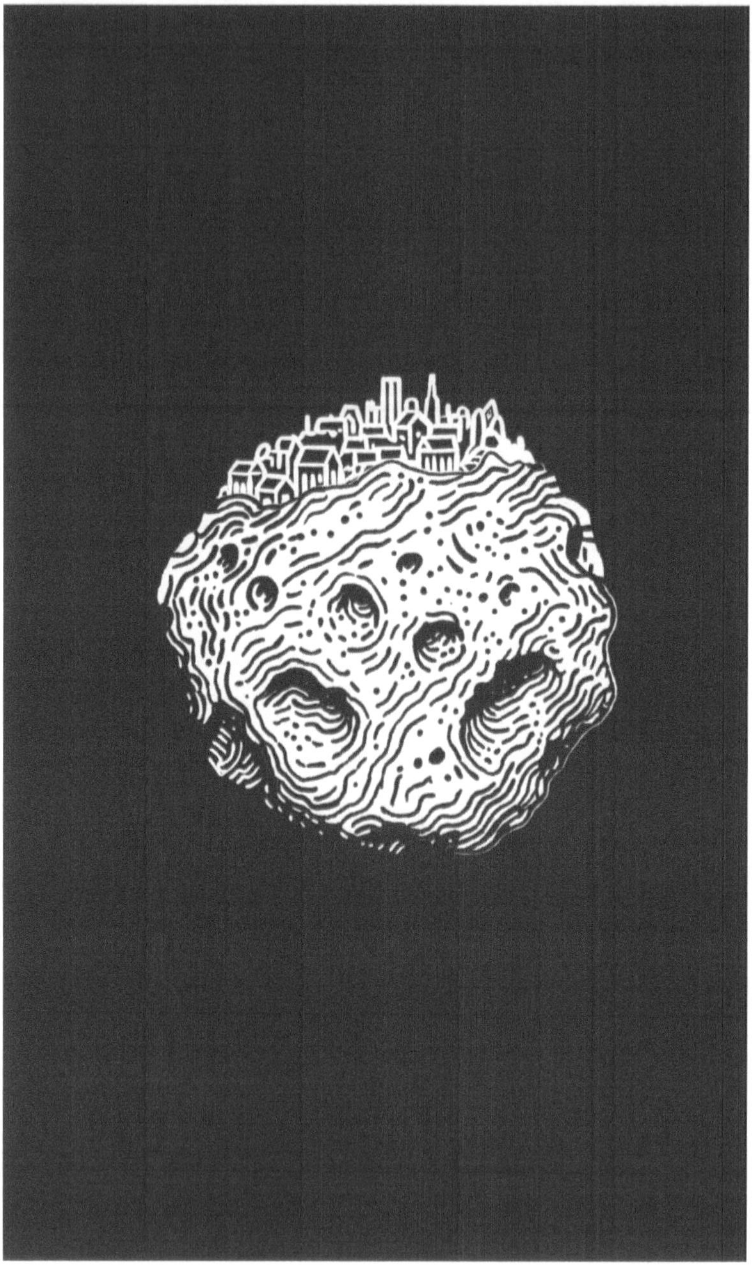

CHAPTER 3

ASTEROWORLD

"There! Do you see it?" Dr. Fester Pacquiano asked his nephew as he looked into the eyepiece of the Observatory telescope.

"Is that Eden? That little dot?" Rocky Pacquiano asked his Uncle Fester.

"Yes! That little pink dot is Eden!" Fester confirmed.

"Are you sure it's not a smudge on the lens or something?" Rocky asked with a smile.

"Haha! very funny," Fester retorted.

"Is that where we come from?" Rocky asked as he pulled away from the eyepiece. His Uncle was no longer there. He looked around, a sense of dread settled in, upon finding himself alone in the circular room.

"THAT IS THE LEADING THEORY!" Fester yelled from behind the shelves as he logged Eden's appearance and features into the records. Rocky breathed a sigh of relief.

The Observatory was a huge dome, with a circular base that contained rows and rows of shelves and a small Processor in the corner. There was a weird clock at the top of the Processor, that kept changing characters if someone looked at it long enough. On the opposite side of the Processor was a Broadcaster, which was showing Cheruball highlights on loop. The center piece of this giant room was however the silver-blue Mya Length Refractor Telescope that peeked out of the dome and into the night sky. The telescope was always staffed by one single attendant in the employ of the Senatorial Laboratories of Elys. Tonight's lone attendant was supposed to be Dr. Fester Pacquiano, but he was soon joined by his nephew Rocky whom he had long suspected had been sneaking out of his classes at Little Eden Junior High, only to drop by at the Observatory to pester his uncle Fester.

"How did you manage to sneak out of the —?" Fester asked calmly as he peeked from behind the shelves at Rocky, who was playing with the Processor now.

"No! No! No!" Fester ran towards Rocky and pulled him away from the keypad.

"I was just trying to look for a better image in the archives, Uncle! I didn't mean to —" Rocky apologized as Fester switched screens and reset the arcane machine.

"This is the better image!" Fester pointed towards the eyepiece of the telescope.

"I don't want to look at a dot! I wanna see how it looks up close!" Rocky protested as Fester felt a bit guilty.

"You can see it with the other Elysians when that clock hits zero! on your BC, at home!" Fester pointed at the weird clock above the processor.

"But I don't wanna wait until the Perihelion!" Rocky protested again as Fester looked at him intensely. His expression softened as he bent down to talk to Rocky at his level.

"We live on Elys," Fester started his explanation. Rocky pouted some more.

"And Elys being an asteroid, rotates differently based on where it is in the orbit. We are predicting the Paradise Observatory, or this Observatory will be the only two, who might be able to capture an image of Eden for the first time, in our history," Fester explained some more. Rocky looked at him with disappointment.

"There is a small chance that this Observatory might completely miss it. That's why I say the BC at your home is probably the best way to look at Eden up close!" Fester continued, as he pointed towards the Broadcaster in the corner.

"If I can't see it on the BC?" Rocky looked up.

"Then I promise I will bring you here, and we will see Eden together!" Fester held out his hand. Rocky smiled and shook it. The niceties didn't last long as their conversation was interrupted by a loud knock on the Observatory door.

"Who is it?" Fester inquired as he looked at the clock on his arm.

"It's Armie! Open up!" the voice from the other side answered.

"Hide! Hide!" Fester whispered to Rocky as he ran for the shelves.

"Coming!" Fester answered after confirming that Rocky was hidden properly.

"Welcome to my domain, Brother!" Fester mocked his brother Armie Pacquiano, as he ushered him into the Observatory.

"Where is Rocky?" he looked around.

"Well! he is not here!" Fester lied as he followed his elder brother's eyes.

"The school said he was not seen after recess. I know he sneaks off to the observatory, to play around with this science stuff!" Armie pointed at the telescope as fury dripped from his face.

"Well, if only you were better at the 'Science Stuff' he would come straight home!" Fester jested as a distant giggle echoed behind the shelves.

"Rocky come out here! NOW! We are going home!" Armie bellowed towards the shelves and then looked furiously at Fester.

Rocky emerged from behind the shelves looking down at the floor. He was still giggling a little as he looked up at the disappointed face of his father.

"Get your bag, we are going home!" Armie ordered Rocky as he scrambled to get the bag from near the door and looped back to collect his trench coat from the chair near the Processor.

They headed towards the door as Armie turned around to look at his little brother.

"Get home before breakfast!" he said, as if it was someone else's order and he was just a messenger.

"Tell Minnie, I will be there!" Fester smiled mockingly as Armie scoffed and exited the Lab.

* * *

The oblong Asteroid Elys was the outermost celestial body in the Dei Solar System. It was home to many settlements that housed over a million inhabitants. The short greyish green Elysians, with their huge eyes and unusually long fingers ambled about their day at a brisk pace, just like any other isolated sentient life in this vast universe. One of these quaint settlements known as Little Eden, was home to the Pacquianos, who lived peacefully in their comfortable dwellings on Darwish Street. Unbeknownst to all of them, their lives were about to change dramatically.

"Happy Perihelion!" Minnie Pacquiano greeted her family as she brought out a huge paddy cake onto the dining table.

Armie Pacquiano, her husband, was busy watching the latest Cheruball match between Little Eden and Paradise City. Rocky Pacquiano, her one and only son, was busy going through a huge picture book that contained hand drawn sketches. Fester Pacquiano, her brother-in-law and resident freeloader, was nowhere to be seen.

"Where is Fester?" she asked as she looked around the table and into the other room.

"Uncle Fester is sleeping!" Rocky answered as he turned the picture book.

"Big Surprise!" Armie mumbled under his breath as Rocky looked at his father.

"Armie!" Minnie snapped at her husband. He shrugged.

"Your father loves his little brother, just like you are going to love your little sister!" Minnie pointed towards the egg nestled near the hearth as she looked lovingly at her son, followed by a disgruntled look at her husband.

"Merry Perihelion, everybody!" a voice distracted all of them as they looked up to see Fester descending from the stairs.

"Merry Perihelion, Fester! Have some breakfast and paddy cake!" Minnie pointed towards the table. Fester walked up and sat down in the chair near Rocky.

"Our first Perihelion! Aren't you excited Armie?" Fester asked his elder brother who was still watching the Cheruball, intently.

"Yeah! Yeah!" Armie waved off Fester.

"It's your first Perihelion too, Uncle Fester?" Rocky asked as he moved his picture book aside.

"Yes! An Elysian gets to see one, maybe two Perihelions, in his entire life, because of the long orbit of Elys around Dei." Fester explained as he scarfed down some paddy cake.

"Woah! Are you excited?" Rocky asked as he jumped up on the chair and started bouncing in excitement.

"Very! Did you finish the picture book I gave you?" Fester asked as he pulled down Rocky, so that he doesn't break anything. Armie loved pointing out that all of Rocky's quirks and mistakes can be attributed to Fester and his destructive methods of scientific inquiry.

"Yeah! I saw the sketches made by previous Observers; they show that Eden has city lights! Is that true Uncle Fester? Will they be able to see our city lights as we go by?" Rocky asked a loaded question.

"That particular illustration was made by Dr. Armando Otung. It was later found out that Dr. Otung, was a heavy user of psychedelics and all his Observations were discarded as invalid data?" Fester answered as he saw Armie's ear perk up at the mention of psychedelics.

"Are you teaching my son, about drugs?" Armie looked away from the Cheruball Halftime Show.

"Psychedelics, are not drugs!" Fester answered, as he shoved more paddy cake into his mouth.

"Anything that makes you not normal, are drugs!" Armie retorted as he completely turned away from the BC.

"You would know what normal is, wouldn't you Armie!" Fester jested as Minnie came back with cups that contained a viscous liquid with white spots.

"Stop fighting like kids, or I will dial your mother?" Minnie warned the brothers.

"Have grandma and grandpa reached Paradise City?" Rocky jumped back into the conversation, leaving his spotted soup.

"Yes! They made it, just in time for the Perihelion Festival," Minnie confirmed with a smile.

"They might be able to see Eden without a telescope, you know!" Fester pointed out to Rocky, whose smile became wider. Armie turned back to his Cheruball highlights.

"Who is winning?" Fester asked Armie.

"The home team is up by —" Armie started explaining.

"Just kidding! I don't care!" Fester mocked Armie's love for Cheruball. A popular sport on Elys which involved hitting balls over the horizon. It was clear that both brothers disliked each other's passions and pastimes.

Minnie scowled from the kitchen as the steam around her egg rose up into the chimney.

"Alright I am off, need to calibrate the telescope for Perihelion, tonight!" Fester announced as he got up from the table.

"Rocky stop shaking the table!" Armie warned Rocky without looking away from the BC.

"I am not shaking the table!" Rocky answered as the walls started shaking and the BC screen went white.

"Outside! Now!" Fester yelled as Armie picked up Rocky and ran outside the house. Fester rounded up Minnie from the kitchen and tried to push her towards the open door.

"The Egg!" Minnie cried as Fester pushed her outside the door into the purple lawn.

"What's going on?" Armie asked Fester.

"I don't know!" Fester answered as another tremor rocked the neighborhood.

* * *

"According to our sources, yesterday's Tremors were a result of the Old Foundation Mine collapsing, due to what the scientists are reporting now was a Hydrate Explosion" the BC Newscaster's voice blared across the Pacquiano's living room as they looked for any damage to the house.

"What even is a Hydrate Explosion? I bet it's those dirty Senators trying to hide something from us," Armie began his rant.

"The methane trapped inside the ice that lines the Mine walls, went off." Fester explained 'Hydrate Explosion' as he looked for cracks on the ceiling, above which his own room stood.

"If you say so!" Armie snapped.

"Do you think I am lying?" Fester looked away from the ceiling, and scowled at Armie, who was still looking at the Newscaster with disgust.

"All of you scientists are in the pocket of the Senators and the Merchant Unions, how can we ever believe anything that comes out of your mouths?" Armie turned around to engage with Fester. This time both stood up to face each other.

"You work for the Merchant Unions, who are you to mouth off, the scientists?" Fester stood his ground as Rocky moved under the dining table.

"Yes I work for the Unions! As an independent contractor, do you know how many hoops I have to jump through to land one job, so that I can put food on the table, while you play around with your toys in that foolish dome you call a lab?" Armie was not backing down as the hairs below his nose twitched uncontrollably.

"That Observation Dome can help us get off this hell-rock and take us back to Eden? Our true home!" Fester retorted.

"Eden, Eden, Eden! That's all you babble about, while the rest of us have to live in the real world, earn real money, put real food on the table and pay real taxes. Most of which you conveniently waste on your ugly Observatories and so-called Space Technology!" Armie thundered as he looked to his side. Minnie was no longer at his side. His anger was replaced with worry as he looked for his wife. He found her in the kitchen, sitting near the Egg, sobbing silently.

"The Egg, I cannot hear his heartbeat — tsk, tsk!" Minnie cleared her nose as Armie sat down and put his arms around her. Fester looked at the egg for a moment and then ran back upstairs. Armie looked at Rocky who was still hiding under the table.

"You can come out now! The tremors have passed," Armie beckoned Rocky to come out from under the table.

"Uncle Fester —" Rocky began to speak, as he was interrupted by a loud thump on the stair landing. It was Fester with a weird gadget in his hand. He moved towards the Egg as Armie got up to stop him.

"Relax, it's just a Delta Ray Scanner, it's used to scan sub surfaces really, completely harmless!" Fester assured Armie as he refused to move away from the Egg. Fester's expression softened.

"It will help me detect the baby's heartbeat!" Fester said with a sincere nod. Minnie held out her long fingers and pulled Armie away as Fester approached the Egg.

He set up a screen on the kitchen counter and connected a wire to the rectangular scanner that he held in his hand. Slowly, he moved the scanner around the Egg, as a soft thump emanated from the screen. Minnie stood up to take a look.

"It's slow, but it's there!" Fester moved the scanner around. Minnie sobbed some more but held Armie's hand as tight as she could.

"I have read in my optional bionomy classes, that gestating eggs can slow down blood flow whenever they are threatened, to make sure the blood loss is minimal before the clot settles in. So, this I believe is completely normal!" Armie pulled away his scanner as Armie let out a sigh of relief.

"So, is the baby going to be okay?" a voice came from the back as all three of them turned around, it was Rocky, holding his picture book.

"Yes, it is going to be okay!" Fester assured Rocky as he dropped the picture book and ran towards his uncle. Fester picked him up and handed him the scanner, so that he can run it around the egg and see for himself.

"What time is it?" Armie asked as he looked outside the kitchen window. Fester looked in the direction his brother was looking as Rocky played around with the scanner. It was dark outside.

"We just had breakfast; how can it be night already?" Minnie mumbled, as she wiped her tears away.

"I need to go!" Fester announced as he put Rocky on the kitchen counter and ran towards the door.

"Where are you going?" Armie asked, with a hint of concern in his voice.

"Eden! I am going to see Eden!" he answered as the door slammed shut behind him.

* * *

Fester ran around the Observatory with a small notepad in his hand. He dashed between the telescope and the processor as he scanned the night sky for Eden. To his dismay the sky remained predictability empty. He slumped down on the chair near the processor and recounted his thoughts.

He was still perplexed about how night came about so quickly. He checked his watch to see that it was still supposed to be daytime. Something was off and he could feel it. He moved back towards the telescope as a violent knock on the door made him jump in place.

"Go away I am busy!" Fester yelled.

"It's me! Armie!" said the voice from the other side.

"I am busy Armie!" Fester replied.

"I am not here to fight, just open the door Fez!" Armie spoke loudly.

"Fez! Fez!" Fester thought to himself as he mouthed a long-forgotten nickname. A feeling of regret washed over him.

He could not remember the last time he and his brother talked without it turning into a fight. Ever since their parents retired and went for the road trip around Elys, Fester had been Armie's responsibility. Considering Armie already had a family, and Fester's job didn't pay much, they came to share the house their parents left them. Armie believed the house must go to him since he had a complete family, and Fester should look for a place closer to his work. This became the first battle in the war of brothers that continues to rage till this day.

It wasn't that Minnie wanted Fester out or Rocky didn't like the company of his uncle, it was that Armie didn't respect his brother's life choices enough and believed him to be a moocher off the hard built family wealth. So many a times Fester threatened to run away and find isolation in a cheap rental high-rises at the outskirts of town, but every time Minnie reminded her husband that Fester is their responsibility and that she made a promise to their parents that she will take care of Fester, before they left for their road trip. Apart from Minnie, only one thing made him stay, his curious and energetic nephew — Rocky, who always looked up to him, in defiance of his own father.

"I have Rocky with me, he wants to talk to you," Armie knocked again as Fester got up on his feet and slammed the notepad on the table.

"What?" he yelled as he opened the Observatory door to find his brother and nephew staring at him.

"They are not showing it! Eden, it's not there, you promised, Uncle Fester!" Rocky sobbed as he held Armie's hand.

"Get inside!" Fester ushered them in as he sat down on his desk.

"It's not there!" Fester said dejectedly as his nose drooped in disappointment.

"What do you mean, it's not there?" Armie inquired as Rocky ran away to check for himself in the telescope's eyepiece.

"Something happened, when those tremors hit, all the other Observatories are reporting, blank night sky as well, that's why they are not able to show it on the Broadcaster," Fester answered as he held his head in his hands.

"I just heard from Mum and Dad, they are okay, the tremors were barely felt in Paradise City," Armie spoke in a low tone as he put his hand on Fester's right shoulder.

"So much time developing the technology to capture Eden's first images, all of it has gone to waste!" Fester mumbled under his breath.

"It's alright, maybe they will figure it out soon — uh— I mean whatever happened!" Armie consoled his little brother as Rocky switched channels to on the Broadcaster hoping to see Eden.

"You don't understand, we will all be dead by the next Perihelion, this was my first and last chance!" Fester retorted as he waited for Armie's usual mocking reply. Instead, Armie just smiled.

"You and I might be dead Fez, but one of us will survive to see Eden next time!" Armie pointed towards Rocky who was back at the telescope tinkering with its dials and eyepiece. A warm feeling erupted inside Fester as he looked up at his brother.

There was another knock on the door, that made all three Pacquiano jump in place and pay attention.

"Are you expecting someone?" Armie whispered as he looked at Fester.

"No!" Fester replied with a hint of defiance.

"Then who is it?" Armie asked, as sternness returned in his voice.

"How am I supposed to know?" Fester whispered loudly.

"I overheard some people in the street talking about how the tremors were caused by the government!" Armie said as he tilted his head forward.

"How is that my problem?" Fester asked annoyingly.

"You work for the government!" Armie answered as another violent knock echoed in the mostly empty Observatory Dome.

"Don't open it!" Armie warned Fester as Rocky hid behind his father.

Fester opened the door to find four individuals in uniform surrounding one small Elysian in a tight vapor suit. Armie walked towards the door as he towered over Fester to take a look at the peculiar new guests.

"We are from the Senate, are you Mr. Pacquiano?" the guy in the vapor suit asked.

"Yes!" Armie answered as Fester opened his mouth to answer.

"We are looking for Mr. Fester Pacquiano!" the vapor suit clarified.

"It's Dr. Fester Pacquiano, and yes I am him!" Fester moved forward.

"DOCTOR Pacquiano, I need you to come with us!" he declared.

"Where, why, who are you?" Fester asked.

"As I said we are from the Senate, and you are needed at the Senatorial Laboratory," the mysterious Elysian replied.

"Senatorial Lab –" Fester mumbled under his breath.

"He asked, who are you, and why do you need him at the Senatorial Laboratory?" Armie was now standing in front of Fester.

"I am Special Agent Jeremiah Arvano, I work for Senator Alezei Zumov, and Mr. — I am sorry — Dr. Pacquiano is required to be at the Lab as soon as possible," the vapor suit answered. Armie turned around to check for his brother but to his surprise, Fester was already already at his desk, packing up.

"What does Zumov need from my brother?" Armie protested, feeling that something was off about the way the agents approached him in the middle of the night.

"It's classified!" Agent Arvano brushed aside Armie's concerns as he looked inside the Observatory to get a good look at Fester. Unluckily for him, Armie's giant frame was blocking the view.

"He will not go anywhere until you tell us what is going on?" Armie protested again.

"As I said —" Agent Arvano began his answer as Fester emerged from behind his older brother. He was wearing his backpack, which was a little more full than usual.

"Armie, you need to take Rocky home and wait for me!" Fester said, calmly.

"No! I don't like the look of these agents, after the tremors and disappearance of Eden, all this secrecy seems very off to me, I cannot let you go!" Armie stood between Fester and the agents.

"Armie, now is not the time to fight, I have to go with them, it's part of my job, I work for the Senatorial Lab, I need to —" Fester tried to convince his brother.

"No! I cannot let you go; Mum and Dad would be —" Armie protested.

"Uhm" coughed Agent Arvano as both brothers turned towards him.

"You can come with us too!" Agent Arvano with a sinister grin. Fester felt threatened and so did Rocky who hid behind him. Maybe Armie is right, maybe these people were not what they claimed to be. The expression on Agent Arvano's face changed from mischievous to calm as he pulled out a file from his bag. It had the seal labelled — 'CONFIDENTIAL | DO NOT SHARE WITHOUT AUTHORIZATION!'

He handed the file to Fester under the arm of Armie who was still looking menacingly at the agents.

"We can arrange for the boy to be dropped home," Agent Arvano said calmly.

"This says we are about to collide into Euphrates!" Fester mumbled from behind Armie as he turned around.

"Euphrates, the planet?" Armie inquired.

"Yes! the giant gas planet," Agent Arvano confirmed.

"What how, uh when?" Armie mumbled confusedly.

"We need Dr. Pacquiano to verify the orbital mechanics on that!" Arvano pointed at the file.

"Armie, Rocky come with me" Fester ordered as he walked past the agents towards their carrier.

"But!" Agent Arvano protested.

"Do you want me to verify these numbers or not!" Fester turned around.

"Yes! But —"

"No buts they go where I go, or I don't go at all!" Fester declared. A smile appeared on Armie's face as he looked down at his son.

Agent Arvano looked at the Pacquianos as his expression changed from confusion to resolve. He signaled his agents to help their three new guests into the carriers, lined up on the lone road that led to Little Eden Observatory.

The carriers started up as they hovered over the barkasmic road. Loud noises filled the air as the vehicles charged up and darted forward one by one.

* * *

"The numbers are correct; we are on a collision course with Euphrates" Fester confirmed to Senator Alezei Zumov. His expression remained unchanged as he signaled Special Agent Arvano.

Alezei Zumov, was born and brought up in the city of Edenson. A small mining town in the last Perihelion, it had prospered to a full-fledged energy state under the Senatorial leadership of Zumov. He wore a monocle and had a long scar on the left side of his face, leading up to some missing facial hair on the same side. He was short but commanded a presence that made everyone realize at once as to who was in-charge.

Zumov was poised to be the next Consul, more conveniently known as the leader of the City States of Elys. But something had happened in the last few days that had endangered his chances for the top job.

"The Foundation Mine Explosion!" Zumov grumbled as a group of Elysians in white coats entered the meeting room situated on the seventh sublevel of the Senatorial Laboratories.

"That is the likely cause!" one of the bespectacled Elysians pointed out.

"How can an explosion change our orbit?" Armie addressed the group of intelligent scientists who crowded the room.

"Who are you?" Zumov turned around to look at the tall frame of Armie, occupying the far corner of the room.

"Armie Pacquiano, Independent Contractor for the Construction Merchant Unions" he introduced himself as Zumov shot a look of disapproval towards Agent Arvano.

"The Foundation Mine was old, older than any other Elysian structure, we have. It ran deep into the heart of our Asteroworld. "Zumov began as he looked away from Arvano.

"When the explosion happened, it ignited a lot of hydrates, creating negative propulsion which destabilized our orbit!" Zumov explained as the mood in the room shifted. Armie squashed down into his chair as he looked outside and waved at Rocky, who was busy watching shuffling channels on the BC.

"We are here to figure out a solution!" Zumov finished his monologue.

"The new axis is off by 2.59 DU" Fester spoke calmly as all heads turned towards him.

"The explosion has also doubled our rotations, so the day-night cycle is now twice as fast! This will have some environmental effects," Fester spoke without hesitation as a sense of panic settled in.

"But we can deal with that. Right now, we need to figure out how to avoid Euphrates?" Fester continued, as everyone in the room listened intently. Armie smiled and nodded as Fester turned towards the board and picked up a green writer.

"Ideas! I need ideas, how can we correct the orbit, while slowing rotations!" Fester asked the room. Nobody spoke.

"Now!" he yelled to drive home his point. Zumov signaled the other scientists as the parade of suggestions started.

"Propulsion Engines!" one of the scientists in the back, pointed out.

"Stupid idea, we don't have enough fuel or time to install and run them!" Fester shot it down.

"Aerobraking!" another voice came from the back.

"Good idea! But we don't know how much atmosphere Euphrates has, for the bounce off!" Fester shot it down too.

"Eject mass, to make Elys lighter!" a scientist in the front suggested.

"Not enough time, can also lead to an unstable orbit!" Fester shot it down.

"Nuclear Propulsion!" another idea came from the group.

"Propulsion of any kind is stupid! Stop repeating ideas!" Fester scowled. Silence. Was he too hard on the crowd of these 'supposed' great minds? Or were they all just pretending to be great? He looked around as everyone looked at the floor.

"Evacuation!" Zumov suggested as he stood up from his seat.

"Evacuate to where and how?" Fester asked the Senator, with the same insolence as he asked the other guys.

"Eden, we have ships —" Zumov began his escape plan.

"Eden! We don't even know if Eden has atmosphere, thanks to the explosion in your mine." Fester looked menacingly at the Senator.

"It's not my —" Zumov spoke up, before Fester started again.

"How can you decide to move a million Elysians there without confirmation!" Fester protested.

"We don't have ships for all of them, only a select few," Zumov looked around the room. Fester felt a pit in his gut. Evacuation was a stupid idea, and evacuating a few on untested ships was somehow even more stupid. He had to do something.

"Eden, has long been believed to be our home planet, sooner or later we have to commit to an escape —" Zumov started another monologue.

"Explosion!" Fester mumbled as he started writing down numbers and equations on the board.

"We have to move on from the mine explosion, it happened, we cannot do anything about it now," Zumov deflected blame as Armie stood up from his chair in the corner.

"I am talking about a new explosion, in the opposite direction. A controlled one this time!" Fester suggested as Zumov leaned in.

For the next few minutes, the bright minds in meeting room W2 of the seventh sublevel in Senatorial Laboratories took a backseat to Dr. Fester Pacquiano, who continued to draw multiple diagrams labelled with arcane measurement values and their units. At the bottom of the board, he wrote — Total Mass of Elys = 1000000000000000000000.

"In the first explosion, that happened yesterday, or two days ago, however you are measuring the time, we lost 11.4 parts of the total mass of Elys, which converted our orbit into a hyperbolic trajectory towards Euphrates, the gas giant," Fester began his explanations, as he wiped off one zero from the total mass.

"If we are to do a second explosion, this one in a more controlled setting, we can reverse the velocity and correct our axis back to a stable orbit." Fester went on.

"How much mass will we lose this time?" Zumov jumped in.

"We would need to lose at least 5 parts of total mass of Elys," Fester wiped half a zero from the total mass value.

"How will this affect the atmosphere, and quality of life on Elys?" Zumov asked again.

"The rotations will increase, the day-night cycle will speed up further and we will have to counter it with more explosions, but it can be managed, after we escape this death spiral into Euphrates," Fester answered.

"I see!" Zumov mumbled as the scientists in the room scribbled away on their notepads trying to verify Fester's numbers.

"We have 1000 days until we crash into Euphrates. We have to trigger the explosion before Day 600, or in this case Day 1200, since the day-night cycle has doubled. But after that we will hit the point of no return!" Fester declared as he completed his calculations on the board.

"How do we trigger this counter explosion?" Zumov asked.'

"We have to build a substructure like the Foundation Mine first to house and direct the explosion" Fester replied.

"And who will build this substructure?" Zumov asked absent mindedly.

"The Merchant Unions" Armie replied, as all heads turned towards him.

"I can talk to the Union members and explain the urgency of the project!" he continued, as Fester gave him a nod. Zumov felt the brotherly connection as he looked up at the board, once more.

"What are we waiting for, let's get to work!" Zumov smiled as the scientists scattered away leaving Zumov, Fester and Armie standing in the middle of the Situation Room.

* * *

It was standard day 527 of building the Imago Dei, a 50-level deep structure in the middle of Paradise City. All the 50 levels were strapped with explosives that were to go off in succession, starting from the bottom.

Most of the inhabitants were moved to Little Eden, which was on the other side of the Asteroworld of Elys. The Unions worked nonstop to make sure there is no splintering, no rogue charges or leaks in the structure. There was an overwhelming possibility that the explosion could get out of control and split their world into two.

"We are done!" Armie reported to Zumov who was in deep conversation with Fester regarding Stage 2 of Imago Dei, where they would try to counter act the rotational forces from the explosion.

"Great work! If it hadn't been for you two brothers, Imago Dei would never have been completed, and we would all be doomed" Zumov patted Armie and Fester on the back.

"When can we trigger the blast?" Fester inquired.

"The final inspections will take, maybe a day or two, once we get the green light from the Mining Union, we can go ahead!" Armie confirmed.

"Good! Make sure the charges don't come loose, if any of them hit the perimeter walls, the direction of the explosion can change," Fester warned Armie.

"I know, I know, I will check the charges myself, all of the timed dry runs have been successful, and the black boxes are doubly lined to prevent interference from other blasts!" Armie assured Fester as Zumov looked down into the endless cavern that extended from the surface and into the center of Elys.

"The heart of Elys!" Zumov mumbled as the Pacquiano brothers looked at him with confusion.

"Did you say something Senator?" Armie asked.

"Nothing! I have arranged carriers for both of you to get back to Little Eden," he said hesitantly as he looked down into the cavern once more.

"I still have some inspections to run," Armie protested.

"The other union members can take care of that, you are heroes of Elys and you must be celebrated as such, I have arranged for a little party back at your old Observatory, before we activate Imago Dei," Zumov smiled.

"I don't —" Fester and Armie started their protests at the same time.

"It is not optional; the Consul is going to be there. We must instill confidence in our people before we take this step!" Zumov interrupted their protests.

"But —" Armie protested once more.

"Ah! here are your carriers, you must get back to Eden now, I will soon follow." Zumov pushed the two brothers towards a Carrier marked with the Senate Seal.

"Something's not right!" Fester declared as Armie sat in the opposing seat.

* * *

"Today marks the day, we take destiny into our own hands," Zumov addressed the people outside the Imago Dei Site, as Fester and Armie watched him on the BC from their home in Little Eden.

"Under my guidance, we have built the Imago Dei. A machine that will save us from our 'inevitable' plunge into Euphrates!" Zumov continued as Rocky, Armie and Fester ate dinner around the table.

"It's not a machine!" mumbled Fester as he looked into the kitchen for Minnie who was cooking up some desserts.

"Where is baby Ari?" Fester asked as Minnie turned around.

"With one press of this button, the machine will start and restore us back into our natural orbit," Zumov's voice blared across the dining room.

"She is upstairs, playing with her toys!" Minnie answered.

"Rocky! Would you please go up and get your sister, it is about to start," Armie ordered Rocky, who was slaving over his notepad.

"I can't I have to turn in this paper tomorrow," a teenage Rocky protested.

"Listen to your father!" Fester reinforced his brother's order. Rocky got up from the table and reluctantly stormed upstairs to fetch his baby sister.

"Mom, Dad, it's starting!" Fester yelled into the living room to fetch Mr. and Mrs. Pacquiano who were trimming the tarmancles off of the house plant.

"Shouldn't we be inside an underground bunker or something for this?" Jeremy Pacquiano, Armie and Fester's father, asked in a curious tone.

"Underground is probably the worst place to be right now!" Fester joked.

"10...9...8...7...6...5...4...3" Zumov led the countdown.

Fester was at the edge of his seat as he watched Zumov's hand move towards a giant red button.

"Click!" a mechanical noise came from the button as Zumov pressed it.

Nothing happened. Everyone in the Pacquiano household looked at Fester and Armie, who were still looking at the inset image of the Imago Dei Site.

There was a flash on the screen as the little inset went completely white. Zumov turned to look at the explosion as the BC screen went dark. Armie and Fester looked at each other.

The first tremor hit within moments as the house rocked violently. Then a distant boom filled the ears as everything shook, and Minnie looked upstairs for Rocky and Ari, who were still not back.

The second tremor hit as a crack appeared in the wall between the kitchen and dining room. Fester and Armie continued to look at each other, a look of horror on both of their faces.

The third tremor struck, and the two brothers exchanged one final glance— whatever was happening, it had only just begun.

CHAPTER 4

TUNNEL

"They refuse to dig further, Sahib!" Survey Assistant Atmaram Patel reported as he entered the Base Camp for the excavation of the Kaknam Stupas.

"What do you mean they 'refuse to dig'?" asked John May, Chief Surveyor of Antiquities for East India Company.

"They believe the Stupas are a holy site and the Buddhist Monks whose spirits reside within the mounds, will curse them and their family!" Atmaram explained as they walked through the base camp towards the Central Tent.

"Don't use the pickaxe you idiot, clean it with the brush first to see where you are digging!" May scolded a local worker, who was digging around a limestone pillar. Atmaram pointed towards the brushes as they walked by a partially dug up temple with long pillars in a covered courtyard and an inner sanctum that was filled with the red soil of the Kaknam Hills.

"Nonsense! You tell those dawdlers that I will pay 8 annas per day, to whoever volunteers to dig first," May turned towards Atmaram as he pushed his index finger into Atmaram's chest.

"It's not a question of money, Sahib. You can pay them in gold, and they will not touch the holy Stupas," Atmaram explained further as they walked past a scaffolding around a giant ornate gateway.

"You lot really know how to take care of your holy sites don't you?" May pointed towards the partially unearthed mounds at the top of the hill. Atmaram let out a dry smile.

"I mean I am just saying, if General Taylor hadn't been hunting that fateful day, he would have never come across your so-called 'holy site'" May continued his rant as Atmaram looked more and more uncomfortable.

"At least that way I wouldn't have been assigned to this god-forsaken place," May vented some more as Atmaram followed him inside the Central Tent. He knew May wanted to be assigned to the recently discovered prehistoric caves in the South. Instead, he was stuck here with the painfully slow task of unearthing some 4th Century Buddhist Stupas.

"All I am saying is, we need to know what's inside those Mounds, otherwise this whole expedition will be sacked, and I will be shipped back to Britain, to work as a back-office clerk " May cooled down as he got out of the scorching sun.

"Let me talk to the workers. I know the elders won't touch it but the offer of 8 annas per day is hard to pass for the younger boys," Atmaram relented as he looked around the Central Tent, which was chock full of excavated artifacts from the dig site. He looked at the open map, which described an incomplete layout of the Kaknam Stupas.

"Hold off on the offer, I still need budget approvals from Maddock for the wage increase. I wrote to him last week; the reply should arrive any day now!" May spoke calmly now as Atmaram looked around the tent for a stool for his boss.

"How goes the work on the Tunnel?" May asked as he sat down and gulped some water from his canteen.

"The entrance is barely visible, but the workers say the inner cavern, is completely traversable! And —" Atmaram reported about the newest structure that the workers found on the west end of the site.

"There is a carving at the entrance, of a Three Headed Elephant!" Atmaram completed his report, as May turned away from him.

"Interesting! Where do you think it leads, though?" May asked as he picked up a pencil and scribbled something on the west side of the map.

"Your guess is as good as mine, Sir," Atmaram said with a hint of reserved smile.

"Come on, Atma, I have known you for over a decade now. I know your tricks, especially the one about interrogating the locals for some juicy native folklore!" May swiveled around to investigate Atmaram's reserved smile.

"Well, I have asked around, nobody knows anything about a Tunnel. Well, except —" Atmaram stopped as May gave him a curious look.

"Except what?" May asked.

"Except an old folk song from Bhilsa. I mean there is seriously no way to confirm it," Atmaram hesitated some more.

"Out with it, man! Maybe it's a way inside those mounds. Governor Maddock has been breathing down my neck for a report, I need to know everything!" May groveled as something rustled outside the tent.

"The song says —" Atmaram began as he was interrupted by a Dak Runner Peon who entered the tent with a stack of letters.

He handed the letters to May, posted a salute, turned around and left.

"Ah! Speak of the devil," May mumbled as he pulled off a letter from Sir Reginald Maddock, Governor of Bengal Presidency and his boss. He picked up his army knife and slit open the envelope. As he pulled out the letter and started reading, his eyes widened with every line reset, bobbing his neck slowly and pulling the paper closer to verify if he read it right.

"What happened, Sahib?" Atmaram asked as concern manifested on May's face. In response, May handed him the letter and headed outside.

Atmaram turned the letter over and started reading.

To the Honorable John May,
Chief Surveyor of Antiquities
Kaknam Excavations

Date: 15th March 1822

Dear John,

The Nizam has refused to pay for the excavation. Henceforth the Treasury has rejected your budget proposals. Halt the digging and clear the site of unwanted personnel. I have authorized a small regiment to travel to Kaknam and use explosives to blow open the Mounds.
The High Command believes the existence of Hellenic Gold is hidden inside the structures. I believe the explosives will only reveal yet more dirt, but we must finish the excavation report.
I count on you to release all the labor force and await further instructions from the travelling Regiment.

Sincerely
Sir Reginal Maddock,
Governor of the Bengal Presidency,
Fort William, Calcutta.

"They want to blow it up?" Atmaram asked May, who had just reentered the tent, after catching some much-needed fresh air.

"I am afraid so!" May confirmed.

* * *

"Have you written to the Governor-General, Sahib?" Atmaram asked as he walked on the scaffolding and inspected the meticulously placed limestones, which shaped the Stupa Mound. The cool summer wind flowed through his hair as dusk approached and he looked at John May, with hope.

"I have, but I am afraid Maddock's Bombing Regiment will be here sooner than the General's reply," May replied as he cleaned dirt off the limestones, in the hopes of uncovering more inscriptions.

"Is there nothing we can do? I mean blasting a piece of history for gold, hardly seems fair, not to mention the revolt and the protests by the locals," Atmaram pleaded as he stepped onto the ladder to get off the scaffolding.

"Where are you going man?" May interrupted their conversation as Atmaram stopped midway.

"It's time for the evening aarti (prayers), Sahib. The wife must be waiting," Atmaram explained as he resumed his descent.

"Can't you skip your prayers for one evening, mate. We must figure out a way to get into these mounds before Mad Dog Maddock's Bombing Regiment arrives!" May explained as he saw Atmaram contemplating his demand.

"Let me call a peon, he can run home and alert the missus," May offered a way out as he pointed the brush in his hand towards the worker camp.

"That's not the problem, Sahib!" Atmaram hesitated.

"Then what is it?" May asked, on the verge of losing his patience.

"It's that, I have never missed an Aarti and –" Atmaram explained his religious routine, before being interrupted by May again.

"Oh, come off it man! Would you rather Maddock destroyed this holy site of yours, or skip one round of evening prayers?" May gave a choice. After a moment, Atmaram started climbing back up again.

"That's more like it, now hand me the chisel," May ordered as Atmaram hesitantly fetched the sharp-edged tool that is used to chip away stone and hardened soil. May saw the shaky hand of Atmaram and looked at him with a smile.

"Don't worry! I am not going to destroy your precious Stupas, I just want to chip away a couple of stones to see what's inside, that way I can convince Maddock to not destroy the whole thing," May assured Atmaram as he slowly chipped at a limestone in the middle.

Evening turned into night, as Atmaram lit a small lantern to assist May with his digging. The entire site was deserted, as May had let go of most of the workers on the orders of Governor Maddock. The only sound that could be heard in the dead of the cool summer night was that of some tumbling cicadas and the thythmic tapping of May's hammer against the chisel pointed at a small cross section of the Great Mound's wall.

"Another layer of limestone!" May said, dejectedly as Atmaram pushed the lantern closer. May was right, there was a fresh layer of meticulously placed limestones visible from the hole that May had just dug in.

"By God! Is anything simple in this godforsaken land," May threw down the tools in frustration and sat down with his back against the Mound.

"We have three Stupa Mounds, we can ask the regiment to blow one of the smaller ones, and if they don't find anything, there is no need for blowing up the rest, right?" Atmaram jumped into problem solving mode. May remained silent; his expression switched from frustration to hopelessness.

"Right, Sahib?" Atmaram reinforced his question.

"It doesn't matter anymore!" May began.

"You don't know Maddock, they call him 'mad dog' for a reason. His regiment won't stop until they find the Hellenic gold!" May said dejectedly.

"Maybe there is no, gold — wait what is this 'Hellenic' Gold?" Atmaram interrupted himself as May straightened up. He looked at Atmaram evasively and then walked past him to the scaffolding ramparts that overlooked Kaknam Valley.

"I read it in the letter too, Hellenic Gold! What is it?" Atmaram asked as May let out a sigh.

"It's a bit scandalous; you might not take this well —" May put forth his excuses.

"'Come on, Atma, I have known you for over a decade now' isn't that what you said yesterday?" Atmaram mocked his boss' earlier remarks. May let out a sigh.

"The higher ups, believe that these mounds, the ornate gate and the pillars are not indigenous," he began.

"Not Indigenous? You mean to say that somebody else built them?" Atmaram asked. May nodded.

"They think this kind of artistry and effort can only be from one source!" May explained further.

"What source?" Atmaram asked, with a knot in his throat.

"Hellenic means Greek! Macedonian to be exact! They think Alexander had them built on one of his deeper expeditions." May concluded as he turned away from Atmaram's shocked face and looked down into the valley.

"That's preposterous, we have stories and inscriptions, from the ancestors, and the songs and the folktales from Bhilsa and uh —!" Atmaram rambled, feeling insulted at the notion.

"That's it!" May exclaimed as he turned around towards Atmaram who was in a state of shock.

"The disrespect and the arrogance. How can you even think for a moment, that we as a civilization wouldn't be capable of doing all this —" Atmaram continued his rant as a wave of excitement ran across May's face.

"Atma! Listen to me mate! The songs!" May was smiling as he held Atmaram by the shoulders. He looked at him with disdain, still feeling the racist insult from the British High Command.

"The old folk song, about the Tunnel!" May shook him some more, to pull him out of his hysteria.

"The Bhilsa Song!" Atmaram mumbled as he understood what May was saying.

"The Tunnel can take us —" Atmaram mumbled.

"Inside" both spoke in unison as a smile appeared on Atmaram's face.

* * *

Atmaram Patel was a model student at Serampore Mission School, Calcutta and had graduated with flying colors in 1812 at the tender age of 16. With his newfound ability to communicate with the ruling British, he set off in search for a job, only to land it a few miles to the East in the newly opened Fort William College.

At the new College he worked as a scribe, who helped translate a lot of local literature into English for the Sahibs to read and understand. It is here that he met a bright eyed, John May, fresh-off the boat from England and ready to learn Eastern Philosophy and History.

May taught him about the Western Civilization, which sparked Atmaram's interest in learning his own history. As John May graduated in 1816, he asked Atmaram to be his assistant and managed to take him everywhere he went.

One day as May was working around a small pillar grid in Hampi, he received communication from the Governor, that he was being reassigned to the recently discovered Kaknam Stupa Mounds in the North. He sent for Atmaram immediately and asked him to join him in Kaknam as soon as possible.

Atmaram, who at the time had travelled back to his village to get married to a girl of his parents' choosing, read the invitation from his dear friend and rushed the matrimonial celebrations, much to the dismay of the elders who had travelled far and wide to attend his wedding.

After travelling by various means, he and his wife arrived at Bhilsa, a small artisan town near the Kaknam Valley. It didn't take him long to find his way to the excavation site atop the three hills that surrounded the valley. A sense of pride and excitement swelled within him as he laid eyes on the partially excavated Stupas for the very first time.

It was the most exciting of times as May and Atmaram worked tirelessly on the dig, for the better part of three years. But now something dark loomed on the horizon as all their hard work hung in the balance. A Bombing Regiment was called in by the hardheaded Governor Maddock to blow open the Mounds after he had failed to convince the local Nizam to fund the excavations. Their future looked bleak until ...

"I can provide you a transcript of the song, we don't have to go!" Atmaram pleaded with May as he packed his things and put them on the saddle of his horse.

"I want to see it for myself!" May retorted as he pushed his Flintlock Pistol into the holster and stowed it onto the saddle. Atmaram looked at the holster, containing a firearm, with reluctant disapproval.

"I hear it's a dance and everything!" May jumped up on his horse with a smile.

"But the regiment —" Atmaram protested.

"They won't be here until next week, we have got plenty of time, now come on mate, we will be late for the show!" May smiled some more.

For hours they rode carefully down the Kaknam Hills and into the farming plains to the West. As May balanced his horse on the Earthen Bunds that separated the two wheat fields, he looked back at Atmaram.

"Not much further, Sahib!" Atmaram assured May.

"I wish we could be here forever; the camp is kind of suffocating to be honest!" May said happily as his horse jumped into the field.

Atmaram smiled as they rode further and further towards the artisan town of Bhilsa. As they rode by the locals selling their wares, May stopped and jumped off his horse to inspect a small store.

"Atma, come look at this!" May picked up something white from a small shop littered with boxes that contained different kinds of talismans and artifacts. Atmaram got off his horse and examined what May was showing.

"It's pure ivory, look at the carvings," May pointed out the carving of a Three Headed Elephant.

"It's the same as the one on the gateway to the Tunnel!" Atmaram exclaimed.

"How can this be possible, we have just unearthed the gates," May mumbled to himself as he picked up some more artwork.

"Maybe the Stupas are not Hellenic after all, huh?" Atmaram mocked May's earlier assumption.

"I never said they were Hellenic!" May snapped back and picked up some more pieces.

"Kitna hua?" he asked the vendor.

"Do anna!" the vendor, a teenage boy who wore nothing but a cloth around his bottom, replied in a listless voice. May pulled out two silver coins and dropped it in the brass container, that was stationed near the wares.

"Your Hindi is getting better!" Atmaram praised May as he realized that he had overpaid for the trinkets. Assuming it to be his generosity and not his poor translation skills, Atmaram smiled and led them back to the horses.

After riding deeper into the village, they arrived at a small hut, that led to a courtyard in the back. The archaeologist and his assistant dismounted and walked into the hut, where an old man stood in their way.

"What?" May asked, looking confused. The old man pointed at his shoes and a small pot near the entrance.

"We must take off the shoes and wash our feet before entering!" Atmaram explained to May.

"What nonsense? I will keep them on, no thank you!" May snapped back. The heat was getting to him again.

"Well then we cannot enter!" Atmaram retorted as a song originated from the backyard. May got up on his heels to see if he can spot the musician, but he was stopped by the old man who now stood between him and the entrance to the backyard.

"Alright! Alright!" he pulled off his shoes and then took off his socks as the old man splashed some water from a pot onto his feet. The cool water made him jump in place before eventually realizing that the pot water actually felt quite refreshing.

"A bit more, old chap, will you?" May asked the old man as Atmaram translated and the old man reluctantly poured some more water onto May's feet.

Feeling renewed they entered the courtyard which was lined with locals wearing their most colorful of clothes. The front was lined with ladies who sat huddled in a semicircle. They all wore bright colored sarees with ornate conch shell necklaces. Behind the ladies were a row of men who were also on their best, with vivacious dhotis (a sort of kilt) and colorful turbans.

The girls in the front giggled and gossiped at the sight of May and Atmaram, both of whom felt underdressed for the moment. In the middle was the most amazing sight of all.

A dark-skinned woman, with a saffron saree (draping) wrapped around her body and a small single-stringed instrument in her right hand. On her hip was another instrument, a sort of animal skin drum that produced a sweet sound, every time she tapped it. Around her ankles was yet another instrument, an anklet that made a buzzing sound whenever she tapped her foot on the ground.

"Her entire body is an instrument!" May pointed out to Atmaram with an impressed smile. She began the story song and the two men from Kaknam listened intently.

mukha per lago nahi neem
nachche rahe har gaon balak

sove nahi par jage rahe
har naam japte rahe vichar

"She talks about a boy, who tasted the Neem Tree, and prayed to the Gods to take the taste away," Atmaram leaned in to explain as the songstress, tapped the drum on her hip. May felt bewitched as he watched the woman, tell stories of old, without any context.

shivam vaishnav jivit hove
tab main aas lagau
karma deen ka prabhu adhikari
sukh sampati ko jeete jaye

"One should not look towards the God's for mercy, but only at their actions. If they are good, they would be happy!" Atmaram explained some more as the songstress broke into a trance. When she stopped, she looked dead into the eyes of May.

karma agar jo satvike hote
jaave gufa main swarg mile hai
karma agar jo nakaratmak
gufa leel jaye jal saman

"She mentions a cave here, where if you were good, you would get to Heaven, and if you were bad, the cave would eat you!" Atmaram translated, as May turned his attention towards him.

"Do you think Heaven means Gold?" May asked as a few faces from the crowd turned around and looked at them with contempt for disturbing the song.

"Can be gold, or can be something else. We don't even know if the Cave is the same Tunnel we dug up!" Atmaram whispered confusedly.

maha erawan karega raksha
agar milega indralok main
sumati gyaan ki kathor tapasya
karte rahe jo deen bandhuwan
gufa kategi do dishaon main
ek disha main swarnim tapasya
dooji disha mein nirdayi hatya

Atmaram fell silent as May looked at him for the recent song's translation.

"What is it?" May asked. Atmaram remained unfazed, he was locked into the words coming out of the mouth of the songstress.

"Huh! She is — uh" Atmaram stumbled.

"She has moved on to another song, this does not concern us, let's go!" Atmaram pulled May out of the courtyard and into the hut.

"She said something bad, didn't she, out with it, now!" May asked.

"The Cave or the Tunnel, will split into two. One path will lead to gold and recognition and the other —uh— " Atmaram hesitated.

"What is it? Where will the other path lead?" May pushed for the answer as the old man at the entrance looked at both the men, arguing in a foreign language.

"The other path will -uh– lead to gruesome death!" Atmaram answered nervously as he looked up at John May.

* * *

It had been two days since May and Atmaram had returned from Bhilsa. The truth about the cave haunted Atmaram more than it did May, who kept pushing for the duo to go in and investigate for themselves.

"We are men of science, why should we believe this lone Songstress!" May told a lost Atmaram as they sat in front of the entrance of the recently excavated mysterious Tunnel.

"You and I both know, the local stories carry merit, we cannot disregard this warning, without due consideration!" Atmaram snapped back as he looked up at the stars.

"Maddock's men will arrive any day now, if we do not find an alternate path into the Mounds, he will destroy everything that we have worked for!" May tried to convince Atmaram.

"I am honored that you value my opinion here! But I have a family, I cannot just abandon them," Atmaram pushed back. May felt alone for a moment. Ever since he landed in India, he always counted on Atmaram to have his back. He never felt alone, in either his adventures or misadventures. His friend Atmaram has always been there for him, guiding him through the colonies with shocking ease. But things were different now for his friend was now a married man, who had his own world to take care of.

"Okay then! I shall go alone!" May declared as he got up on his feet.

"Didn't you hear what she said, either you will get gold, or you will die a gruesome death!" Atmaram snapped as he stood up to face his boss.

"There is half a chance that I will find the gold. I will take those odds," May snapped back as Atmaram looked at him with frustration.

"I will not let Maddock and his men destroy my life's work!" May declared, as Atmaram's expression remained unchanged.

There were no words exchanged between the two, as Atmaram picked up his toolbox and walked away.

* * *

The next morning, John May prepared his rucksack in the Central Tent. He was wearing the Explorer's khaki shorts and shirt, tucked nicely away under a toolbelt. He put in all his tools and some rations. He also stuffed in two canteens of water on top a small bottle of lamp oil. He turned around to pick up the lanterns and his hard hat, but his rucksack was gone. He looked around in confusion and then stepped out of the tent. Someone now held his rucksack on his back.

"Couldn't stay away? Could you mate?" May smiled.

"Your chances of death might be lower, if I am with you!" Atmaram smiled back.

"True that man!" May punched his shoulders as the two archaeologists headed West.

They walked into the ornate gateway, across the Stupa Mounds, and finally arrived at edge of the hill, where the Tunnel's entrance awaited them. Atmaram dropped the heavy rucksack on the ground and pulled out the compass.

"We must always turn Northeast, if we want to go for the Mounds!" he pointed towards the Stupa Mounds in the distance. May put on his hard hat and put it on as he adjusted the hem of his shirt. Atmaram picked up the sack and followed May into the cave.

After a few steps in, the sunlight ran out. Atmaram pulled off the two lanterns and ignited them as he handed one to May while holding the other for himself.

The ground was uneven and May kept running into spiderwebs which inevitably stuck to his hard hat like a spaced out fabric. After walking for what felt like an hour, Atmaram looked at the compass. They were still headed Northwest.

"Did you hear that?" May turned around.

"Hear what?" Atmaram asked.

"It sounds like —" and before May could finish the sentence, a fluttering sound filled the cave as Atmaram dropped the rucksack to fight off the incoming hoard of bats.

"Bloody hell! Do you know what this means mate?" May smiled as he fought off the bats.

"What?" Atmaram asked as he grabbed the back of his neck.

"There is a way out! The bats must be coming in from somewhere!" May declared as he picked up the oil lamp to illuminate the cavern around him. It was still just walls paved with limestone.

"Or they might just be coming in through a hole, in the side of the hill!" Atmaram retorted, as he picked up his rucksack and lantern.

"Always the killjoy!" May mocked, as they started walking again.

"Did you get bit too?" Atmaram asked as he saw blood on his hand.

"Yeah, I think I got nicked on my leg!" May showed a small blotch of blood below his knee.

"Never mind! "Let's keep moving," May ordered as they walked deeper and deeper into the cave.

In a few minutes, the cave got shallower, and their hard hats scraped the limestone roof. Every few minutes or so another cloud of bats enveloped them, as May braced for impact and

Atmaram used the rucksack to shield himself from a head on collision.

"I am getting sick of this!" May winced.

"I think we are still headed in the right direction," Atmaram checked his compass.

"But we seem to be going deeper into the hill, we should have found the entrance to the Mounds by now!" May noted as they crouched lower and lower to give way to the roof.

The space around them became tighter and tighter as they were almost crawling to get through. And as if things couldn't get worse, May just disappeared. Atmaram's stomach dropped as he let go of the rucksack and crawled faster.

"No! No! No!" May's voice echoed from the front as the crawlspace ended and a dark abyss turned into a steep drop.

Atmaram plunged into a pond as he reached around for help. But before he could spread his legs to swim, he just stood up. The tight tunnel had given way to an enormous cavern which was filled with a layer of knee-high water. He stood back up and looked up at the point at the crawlspace.

"That must be over 15 feet! Good thing the water broke my fall!" May noted as he waded through the water.

Atmaram pulled the rope he attached to his toolbelt earlier and the rucksack fell into the cavern. He caught it just before it touched the water.

"Didn't want the rations to get wet!" Atmaram let out a dry smile, as he looped the sack around and put it on his back.

"I think I found where the bats were coming from," May pointed at the roof of the cavern where an uncountable number of bats hung upside down, twitching slightly here and there. He shuddered as he took his eyes off the roof and walked around the enormous cavern.

"This must be some kind of a sewage system!" May mumbled as he turned around to see Atmaram, refilling the canteens with cavern water.

"Or it can be an escape route, for the monks?" Atmaram hesitated and then continued to refill.

"Whatever it is, it was definitely manmade. Here!" May's voice echoed in the cavern.

"Come take a look at this," May spoke as he moved towards a cavern wall.

"It's the Three Headed Elephant, Erawat" Atmaram exclaimed as he moved in for a closer look.

"This thing has a name?" May exclaimed as he took off his hard hat.

"Yes! Also known as the King of Elephants, it serves as the primary vehicle for Indra, the King of Gods" Atmaram explained as May scratched his head.

"Okay, all I heard was 'King' and that sounds like 'gold' to me," May smiled and put his hard hat back on as they looked for a way forward.

"Over here!" Atmaram pointed to an opening between the rocks that was lined with irregular patches of limestone.

"And it continues!" May ushered in Atmaram, as they walked into the Tunnel.

They walked for few more minutes before they saw something that they were both dreading, since the moment they heard the songstress.

The tunnel had split into two, giving way for two paths forward.

* * *

"The Songstress was right!" Atmaram mumbled as he sat down on the ground and held his head.

"Whoever told her the story must have survived right? We just have to find our way out," May assured Atmaram as he looked at the two paths in front of him.

"Maybe we can go back the way we came in," Atmaram asked May as the English Surveyor walked around and looked back at the way they came in.

"The drop was too steep; I don't think we'll make it. We have to push forward," May retorted as Atmaram looked at the walls for carvings.

"No more limestone walls, no more carvings, we are definitely in a cave now!" May noted as Atmaram looked around some more.

"Get ahold of yourself mate!" May grabbed Atmaram as he saw a deep fear in his eyes. Fear of a man condemned, who was trying to hustle his way back to life. May stepped back. The realization of his ill-fated decision dawned on him. The Songstress was right. One way will lead to gold and the other to gruesome death. Either way they had no way of knowing which one to choose, since both the paths curved North East in the direction of the Mounds.

"No!" May snapped back.

"We have to choose our path and stick to it!" May ordered Atmaram, who was now curled up on the floor once again.

"What if we choose wrong?" Atmaram muttered with bated breath.

"According to that quack Songstress, if you have done good things you will end up happy right?" May asked the panicking Atmaram, who reluctantly nodded.

"You are the most noble person I know, so I believe if we each took one path you are definitely getting the gold!" May assured Atmaram, completely disregarding the image of a possible gruesome death in the name of science.

"But, what about you?" Atmaram asked hesitantly.

"If I do die, just make sure they know my name!" May smiled as he swallowed a knot.

"*maha erawan karega raksha, agar milega indralok main*" Atmaram mumbled to himself as May turned around and peeked into the caves. He looped back to grab the compass from the rucksack.

"Both the paths curve towards North, if we each take one. We can find the exit and call for help!" May suggested as Atmaram looked up at him. His eyes hoped for any alternative.

"Do you have a better plan, I mean we can't go back, we have to push through!" May pleaded to the survivor inside his Indian colleague.

"I will take the right!" Atmaram stood up and grabbed a lantern.

"What about the supplies, I mean the rucksack!" May called out, but Atmaram had already walked into the right cave, without the rucksack.

"I guess I will go left then!" he picked up the rucksack and walked into the right path before watching Atmaram disappear around the bend.

* * *

Atmaram had never met his wife before his wedding day. One day as he worked with John May in the grids of Hampi Excavation Site, he got a letter from home, asking him to be ready for marriage in the next full moon and a week later he left for home.

On the night of his wedding, he received a mysterious letter. It detailed his next posting, in the Kaknam Hills, where some British General had noticed some man-made mounds while he was on a hunt. His job was to assist the newly promoted Chief Surveyor John May, in completing this exciting new dig.

A workaholic by nature, Atmaram found himself a changed man after marriage. He spent more time at home as he got closer to his wife and his gods. He attended the evening prayers regularly and made sure to leave home with a hearty breakfast. After working for 10 years with John May, he had made up his mind to retire after the excavation work for Kaknam Stupas is complete.

A retirement into the farm life now felt like a distant dream to Atmaram as he walked slowly towards his possible death. His only chance was that somehow May chose the path of death.

He dispelled the thought in the favor of getting help as soon as he gets out, or if he gets out. The cave wasn't narrow like before as he walked with a steady pace. He looked around to see what was around him. It was just rocks and nothing else.

A few minutes later he stopped, as his footsteps echoed louder than usual. By the sound of it, he realized that he was in yet another cavern. He swung around his lantern to find a wall, but all he felt was stones. Arranged stones, meticulously arranged limestones!

"Limestones!" he mumbled to himself as he realized he was finally inside one of the Mounds.

"But which one?" he wondered to himself as he walked forwards to the increasing echo of his steps. He theorized that if the echo kept increasing meant he was walking towards the center.

He walked and walked before stopping in the middle of the mound. He swung his lantern around some more. There was no gold in this chamber.

"Maybe the gold is stored near the walls!" he thought to himself as he started walking towards the opposite wall. He saw something.

He swung his lantern in its direction. Whatever it was, it reflected light.

"Gold!" he realized as he broke into a run.

Halfway through he tripped on something sitting on the floor as he fell face first into the ground and passed out.

* * *

John May joined the British Army in the year 1800. He was immediately shipped out to fight the French in Egypt. After an all-out attack, which was later termed as the Battle of Alexandria, the British came out on top, and the French surrendered without conditions.

As Corporal John May, became Lieutenant John May, he oversaw the peaceful withdrawal of the French and handover of many stolen artifacts. The most notable among them was the Rosetta Stone.

A stone slab that was inscribed with three different scripts, it was enough to awaken the explorer within May. After the French Surrender he traveled back to Manchester and enlisted in the East India Company which shipped him out to Calcutta to learn the art of archeology as well as the local language.

After years of dig work under draconian Chief Surveyors, May had the Southern Caves Excavation in his sights. He assured his assistant and longtime friend Atmaram Patel that the posting for the Cave work will come any day now.

All his dreams were shattered when he was instead assigned to some ordinary mounds atop some insignificant hills in the North. He wrote to his trusty sidekick and left at once, hoping to rush the dig so that he can qualify for the Southern Caves.

The rush job was anything but quick as he and his assistant toiled away at Kaknam Dig site for three years only to be replaced last minute by a pack of explosives.

John May had now descended into the mysterious Tunnel that he initially thought would lead him to the inside of the Mounds. But now, his only hope was for a way out.

He walked on the uneven surface carrying the rucksack that his assistant was supposed to be carrying. He held the lantern down below to look for sharp rocks in his path. Soon the path became smooth

"Almost too smooth." he thought as it all happened in an instant.

The floor shuddered beneath his feet, and he fell for what felt like a minute. Luckily his rucksack broke the fall and after much rolling around he managed to get back up on his feet. His lantern was smashed to pieces. He opened the rucksack and pulled out the backup lantern and some lamp oil. He poured it into the lantern and lit it.

He now stood on the same smooth surface, that gave way above him. He swung his lantern around to get his bearings, before stepping forward.

"Huh!" he mumbled as he looked around. There was nothing around him except...

"What was that?" he swung his lantern once more to see what he saw earlier. It was something shiny and big. He walked closer as the realization of the moment dawned upon him.

It was a giant reclining Buddha made of solid gold. He swung around his lantern some more to inspect the base where he saw a small trapdoor.

"That must be the way out!" he mumbled to himself as he pulled out his chisel and hammer. He walked to the foot of the statue and chipped away some gold to convince the outsiders and Maddock's regiment of his finds.

He looked around some more before finally deciding that except for the reclining Buddha, there was nothing in this mound.

"Atma!" he thought to himself as he realized that his dear friend was now heading towards gruesome death. He picked up his rucksack and opened the trapdoor at the base of the statue.

He climbed down into the chambers beneath and crawled all the way to another trapdoor that was already broken. He pushed his way through, and fresh air rushed into his lungs.

He had made it out. With the evidence for gold inside the mounds, he dropped the rucksack and ran for the worker camps.

"I need two people with me, now!" he roared at the crowd of workers who were packing up to leave.

"I will give 10 rupees to the volunteers for half a day's work!" he made a quick calculation in his mind to account for the time it will take him to reach Atmaram. Two young men dropped their sacks and picked up their pickaxes.

"Marvelous! Follow me!" he ordered the two volunteers.

The trio rushed towards the Tunnel and headed in. There were no bats this time as May kept warning the two young workers about the dangers of bat bites.

"Careful! There is a drop!" he remarked some more. Sure enough, there was a drop into the cavern as the three men carefully dropped into the knee-high water of the cavern.

"This way gentlemen!" May was aching to reunite with his friend and tell him all about the solid gold reclining Buddha.

As they approached the split in the cave, May's heart sank as he gazed upon what lay in front of him.

There was no split, in fact the Tunnel just abruptly ended with a huge rock wall, at the top of which was a small hole.

Through the small hole, came two bats and passed the three men on their way to the cavern behind them.

"Did I miss a turn?" he thought to himself as he turned around to explain the situation to the two men, who had followed him down on his second trip.

To his surprise, the two men had disappeared.

* * *

Atmaram opened his eyes as he now found himself in a paddy field. He got up as the water that had soaked him, dried up in an instant. In the distance he saw something majestic.

"*Airavat!*" he exclaimed as a large three-headed white elephant stood behind the hill to his North. Behind the elephant was an even larger majestic palace, that stretched all the way up to the sky.

"*Indralok!*" he muttered as he got out of the fields and looked towards a beautiful pathway to a distant small village.

"*karma agar jo satvike hote, jaave gufa main swarg mile hai*" he remembered the songstress' second prose. This means that there was never any gold, but heaven that awaited him at the end of the Tunnel.

He was home. He had made it to his heaven. As the realization dawned upon him everything went dark.

Atmaram woke up in darkness as the lantern beside him flickered gently. He looked around to see only darkness. He picked up his lantern and realized the heavens were just a dream. He moved the lantern to take a look at what he stumbled upon.

He let out a scream as he slinked back in horror. It was a skull that lay at his feet. He had stumbled upon a sitting dead body.

"You knowingly disturbed my peace!" a voice hissed in his mind. He looked around to find the source.

"A gruesome death awaits!" the voice said, mockingly as the ground beneath him rumbled.

Atmaram screamed as something fell on his leg. It was the limestones that lined the interior and the exterior of the Stupa. The Mound that he was in was collapsing. Another rock fell on his shoulder as it broke his shoulder which held him up right.

The pain was unbearable as another rock fell onto his stomach and blood spurt out from his mouth. He laid there screaming for what felt like hours before a rock finally fell on his head and darkness engulfed him again.

* * *

Piyush Verma got off the bus to join the rest of his class on the field trip to Kaknam Stupa Heritage Site. He pushed past his classmates and reached the front of the pack only to run headfirst into someone.

"Be careful son!" a voice spoke from above as he looked up to see a man with a large moustache smiling at him. Piyush stepped back to get a better look. The mustachioed man was eating paan (leafy mouth freshener), which made his teeth a reddish shade of orange. He also had a badge stuck to his breast pocket that read —

Joseph Fernandes,
Tourist Guide,
Ministry of Tourism & Culture, Government of India

"Today we explore the Kaknam Stupas, and I tell you all about the history of this place!" he said in broken English.

Piyush felt excitement like never before. He had already researched the entire site, with the help of his father. He had read about the Great Emperor who had built the place to promote Buddhism. He had read about the Monks who might have lived and meditated atop the same hill, that he stood on right now.

But soon, all his excitement waned as the Guide became more busy chatting up the female teachers from his class rather than explaining the different structures. He decided to break off from the group and do his own research as he walked up to several structures and read the small plaques that detailed that particular artifact.

After making sure his teachers were still unaware that he was missing, he ran across the grounds to inspect a small structure that barely peeked from the ground. As he approached, he realized that it was a closed off gate to something down below. He read the plaque beside.

ENTRY PROHIBITED

Here lies the Escape Tunnel for the Buddhist Monks, who used it in times of war to escape from the invaders. The tunnel exit is a mystery to this day. Two brave men attempted to solve this mystery in 1822, as Chief Surveyor John May and his Indian Assistant descended into the tunnel and sadly never came back out.

Piyush stepped back to look into the dark tunnel. He edged closer to the barricaded gate, to see if he could listen to someone inside.

"Piyush Verma!" a voice came from above him. It was his class teacher who had broken away from the flirtatious guide and was now furious at Piyush.

"Sorry Ma'am!" Piyush apologized as he moved away from the Tunnel and walked towards a broken Mound.

"What happened there?" he asked his teacher.

"I don't know, let's ask the guide!" his teacher deflected. They approached the sleazy guide.

"Oh yes madam, Governor-General Maddock, who was the Governor of that time, blew up this Stupa in search of gold," the guide excitedly explained in his broken English as Piyush's class teacher let out a weak smile.

"Did he find it? The gold?" Piyush asked the guide, whose smile faded as he looked down at Piyush.

"No gold! All they found were the remains of some Buddhist Monks, around which the mounds were created by their disciples!" the Guide explained, with a reluctant smile.

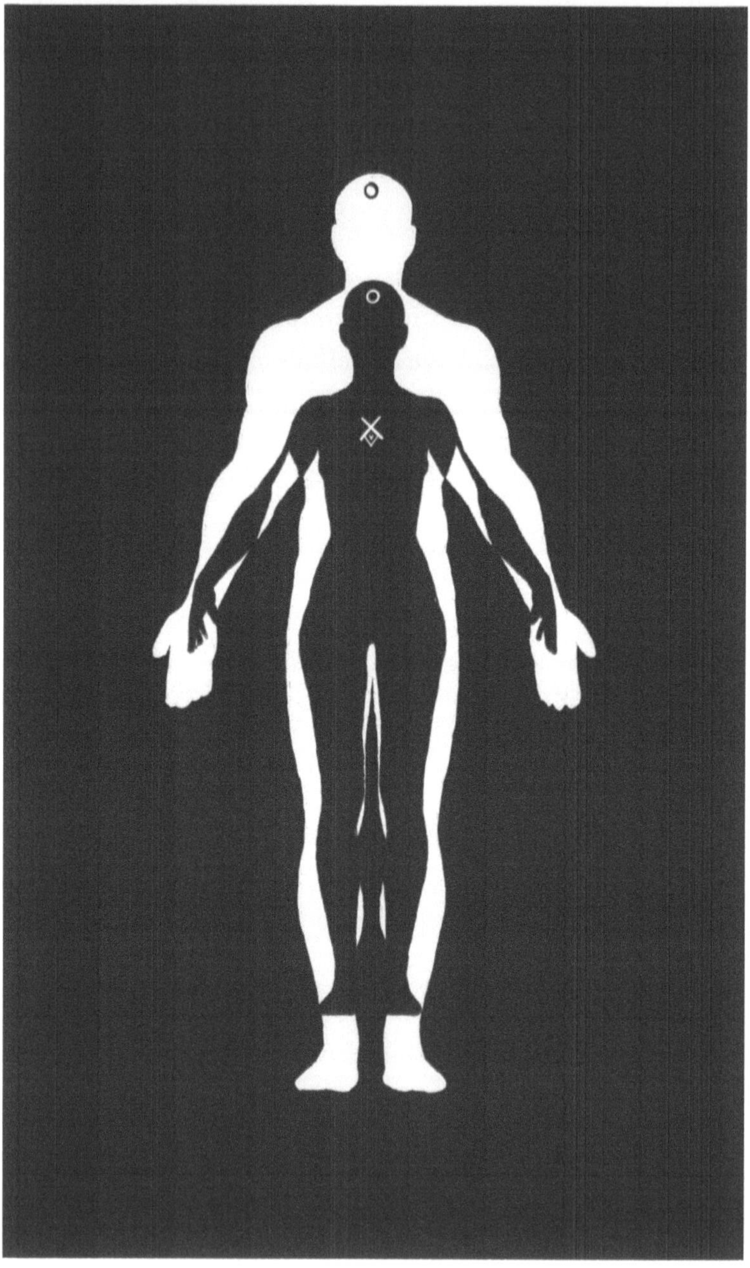

CHAPTER 5

REPLACEMENT

"I am afraid your daughter has something called Pediatric Glioblastoma" Dr. Sommai informed Chayaphon Pugkhem as he sat down in her Pediatric Oncology Office on the fourth floor of Baiplew General Hospital.

Mr. Pugkhem who was colloquially known by his peers as just 'Phon', wore an expression of confusion and distress on his face as the doctor explained the diagnosis.

"What is this Pediatric Globs —?" Phon asked as he looked down at the blindingly white hospital floor. It was evident that he hadn't slept well in the past few days.

"Pediatric Glioblastoma! It's a form of cancer," Dr. Sommai corrected Phon, in a low voice. Phon straightened up in his chair and looked up at the doctor.

"It is rare, but moves immensely fast, especially in kids. In her current state, she has a couple of months left, maybe half a year," Dr. Sommai continued as all color drained from Phon's face.

"But she just fell, one moment she was playing and the next –" Phon stopped to swallow the knot that had formed in his throat.

"It usually presents as headaches or nausea. The fact that she fell and had a full-on seizure prompted us to dig deeper. That's when we found the cancer!" Dr. Sommai explained as she moved a glass of water towards Phon.

"Is there a treatment, what can we do?" Phon struggled with this newfound reality as he felt a thousand needles pierce his back.

"I am afraid the cancer has metastasized, and we are left with very few options!" Dr. Sommai informed Phon who looked at her with an expression of deep shock and resentment. He felt in the moment that it was somehow the doctor's fault that her daughter was dying.

"Stop being stupid!" he thought to himself as he held back tears, waiting for the doctor to explain the treatment options. The room felt small, and a deafening ping settled in his left ear.

"We have limited options" Dr. Sommai began. Phon nodded as a glimmer of hope returned to his face.

"All of which are equally dangerous and do not guarantee a good quality of life post treatment!" she underscored as the hope on Phon's face disregarded Dr. Sommai's disclaimer. She waited for a hint of hesitation or a simple nod, but nothing came as Phon stared with an inch of hope.

"We can introduce something called Adapting Laminaoma, it's a form of slow growing cancer that will redirect the resources away from the Glioblastoma and add months or even years to her life," she explained as Phon's heart sank a little lower.

"You want to give another cancer to my daughter?" Phon asked, as he tried to reconfirm what he had just heard.

"Yes! but it's a slow growing cancer which forms layers around the brain that compete with the GBM –" Dr. Sommai tried to explain before being interrupted by the shocked father.

"What are the chances that she will die from this?" Phon asked as another knot formed in his throat.

"She will die, regardless, Mr. Pugkhem. We are just trying to make sure she gets a little bit more time with you!" Dr. Sommai explained as tears welled up in Phon's eyes. Life felt shorter and all the plans that he had for his career as a Lawyer, now seemed pointless.

"This cannot be it, there must be something you can do, I have heard Chemotherapy and Surgery can —" Phon presented his naive options as the doctor shook her head.

"The cancer has progressed too far, we cannot perform a surgery without killing her or at least paralyzing her, we cannot —" she explained as he looked at a helpless father, wordlessly begging for help. She stood up, walked to her office door and looked outside. There was no one in the hallway since it was 2 AM in the morning. She closed the door and walked back to her desk where a distressed Phon was holding his face in the palm of his hands.

"There is, uh, another option!" she stuttered as she sat back down. Phon looked up.

"We cannot do anything for her in her current state," she began as he saw him perk up.

"What do you mean her current state?" Phon inquired.

"I mean her current body, it's too far gone!" she explained, as another knot travelled down Phon's throat. She waited for him to interrupt her, but when he didn't, she continued.

"We can get her a new body!" Dr. Sommai proposed as Phon looked around him to make sure he heard her right.

* * *

Total Somatic Replacement or TSR for short was developed by Dr. Anay Patel in 2065. A surgeon by profession in the bustling metropolis of Sonos, in Southern Eurasian Territories, Dr. Patel came up with the procedure which involved harvesting compatible organs from multiple donors to reconstitute a functional human body.

This treatment was meant to be used in terminal patients, who cannot go on with their current body. Unfortunately, its misuse started immediately as it was used to extend the lifetimes of the people who could afford it and shorten the lifetimes of those who can't. It was forcibly outlawed in the year 2095, owing to its criminal usage and an out-of-control black market donor economy.

"The procedure can be approved, for exceptional cases, where the patient is exemplary. I mean no alcohol, no drugs, no criminal charges —" Dr. Sommai explained to Phon and his daughter Siri, who lay in the hospital bed, as multiple tubes and monitoring cables flowed from her into a huge display to her left.

"She is 10!" Phon interrupted, as he pointed towards his daughter Siri, who was heartily enjoying her television shows.

"I know! That's what makes her the perfect candidate, I mean the total biomass replacement is less, and the memory mapping itself..." she trailed off as she mumbled to herself.

"Dr. Sommai!" Phon brought her back as she looked up and smiled at the concerned father.

"Mr. Pugkhem, if you would just sign these consent forms for the TSR, I will get started with the organ hunt," she pushed the form towards Phon.

"You look – uh – excited!" he said, as he signed the TSR form.

"A case like this, it's rare! The last TSR was performed over a decade ago, in Bosphorus. I mean the case study alone on this case would be —" Dr. Sommai explained excitedly.

"Is he still alive?" Phon asked before she could trail off again.

"Who?" she turned towards him from the depths of her excited thoughts.

"The patient, in Bosphorus?" Phon asked.

"Oh yeah!" she opened her tablet and sifted through multiple screens.

"There it is!" she mumbled as she pushed one of the documents to the top of the screen and it opened up on the empty space on the giant health monitor screen.

"Mrs. Shirochenko, age 35, diagnosed with Systemic Sclerosis, multiple organ failure and hardening of skin. This is her before the transplant, " she pushed up a picture of the patient. A middle-aged woman with scaly white skin, pale blue eyes and a large mole above her eyebrows. She was covered in tubes and monitoring cables much like Siri. She looked defeated and in immense amount of pain, with the wincing expression she bore, as a doctor held her arm in place for the photo.

"Annnd this is her after the transplant," she pushed another picture. This time of a black woman, with no hair and a smile that stirred something deep inside Phon.

"But she looks —" he interrupted Dr. Sommai.

"Different! Yes, that is a possibility. TSR does not guarantee the same outward appearance. It only makes sure that the person inside is the same person who underwent the procedure. See the mole above her eyebrows," she pointed towards the two pictures of Mrs. Shirochenko, both of which had a large mole above the eyebrows. Phon nodded as he saw the similarity.

"They make sure that one distinguishing feature remains after the procedure. It can be a birth mark, a scar or even a tattoo, that can eventually be used in the Identity Transfer," she explained as the smile refused to leave her face.

"She won't look the same?" Phon asked as something dropped in his stomach, as he looked at Siri, with her beautiful brown eyes that she got from her late mother.

"I will try to make sure the prep team transfers as many features of Siri as they can, but to answer your question, NO! we cannot guarantee that she will look the same!" she said, with a hint of remorse. Phon remained silent.

"She will still be Siri, all her memories and habits, they will all transfer to her new body," Dr. Sommai added to which Phon just stared silently at Siri, who had just fallen asleep, with the wall-mounted TV still on.

"Look at it this way, she is young, she hasn't really created an identity for herself. She will adjust into her new body and become this new person. We can schedule some psych sessions, to guide her through this emotional transition and she will feel like herself again," the doctor continued as Phon got up and peaked through the curtains across the glass walls and into the hospital hallway.

"It's not her that I am worried about!" Phon mumbled as his own reflection in the glass wall stared back at him.

* * *

The Siam Consulting Group, headquartered in the vibrant Baiplew City of the Southeast Eurasian Territories, employed an army of consultants who worked hand in hand with some of the largest conglomerates and governments around the world to solve specific organizational problems. These consultants slipped up from time to time, so to cover these eventualities, SCG also hired an elite unit of lawyers who were meant to drag out these consultants from the tricky situations they got themselves into. One of these elite lawyers was now working from home. Well to be more exact, he was working from a hospital.

Mr. Chayaphon Pugkhem, typed away on his work laptop in the corner of a private hospital suite in Baiplew General. The television opposite the hospital bed blared loudly as Siri, laughed and gasped at a movie starring one of her favorite actor/popstar – Sai Lee.

Multiple notifications popped up as he pushed a haphazardly completed document labelled – Acquisition Compliance Report: AngelShark and Orca International.

As he rushed to answer the numerous questions that his worthless colleagues posted, which they considered an honest day's work, the private room's door slid open and Dr. Sommai walked in. She looked happy, but with a hint of hesitation on her face.

"We have managed to procure, most of the organs, including the skin from a recently deceased girl who died of a drug overdose —" Dr. Sommai announced excitedly as Phon looked at Siri.

"Will you turn that down?" Phon barked at Siri, as he put away his laptop. Dr. Sommai stepped back. Phon immediately regretted his behavior. The stress of the job combined with the uncertainty of Siri's health problems was pushing him in overdrive. He wished in that moment for someone to speak, so that he could stop feeling like a horrible father to a dying child. Thankfully, Siri spoke up.

"But it's Sai Lee, Páa. It's his latest movie. He plays a police—" she began explaining.

"I understand Siri, but the good doctor is here, don't you wanna talk to her?" Phon softened up, which made Dr. Sommai smile again as she approached the bed.

"But –" Siri protested.

"I will buy you those action figures!" bribed Phon.

"Sai Lee and the Barmy Bear!" Siri exclaimed.

"Yes! that one!" confirmed Phon as Siri muted the TV and pushed herself up to welcome Dr. Sommai.

"Hi Pokkie!" she waved at Dr. Sommai.

"Hi Siri!" she waved back as Phon looked at both of them in confusion.

"She gave me the nickname, when she realized I remind her of the famous Butterbear Pokkie!" Dr. Sommai explained to Phon, who let out a forced smile.

"As I was saying! We have most of the organs, they need to be reprocessed and re-engineered to fit Siri's frame, but the initial estimates suggest the metabolic age to be around 19 years old!" Dr. Sommai explained as she pulled out her tablet.

"I am sorry, if I missed it earlier, but did you say you got the skin from a drug overdose girl?" Phon asked as she shifted in his chair beside Siri's bed.

"The drug was ingested nasally, and most of the damage was to the heart, which we have discarded. The skin remains in perfect condition —" Dr. Sommai explained as she smiled through it all hoping to receive a similar reaction from Phon. Instead, he just nodded confusedly.

"We hope to do the transplant within the next month, as the only missing organs are the heart and the pancreas!" she added to her original announcement.

"Good!" Phon said calmly as he looked away.

"There is another thing!" Dr. Sommai hesitated as Phon turned his attention back.

"The latest scans show that the Glioblastoma is progressing faster than we expected!" she began, as Phon straightened up.

"I want to recommend a chemically induced cryogenic coma," she continued.

"A coma?" Phon interrupted her as she looked at Siri, who was now watching the Sai Lee movie on mute.

"Yes! This will slow down the cancer and give us time to preserve the brain for the TSR" she explained as Phon looked at Siri and then at the TV.

"Perhaps we should talk outside," Dr. Sommai suggested as Phon nodded and they headed outside.

"I know coma seems like a big step, but we want to make sure we get to the TSR, without any complications," she spoke in whispers as she smiled and waved at Siri through the glass wall.

"But her movies, she loves them, how can she?" Phon stuttered.

"She can watch those movies, once she transfers into the new healthy body!" Dr. Sommai smiled.

"But —" Phon protested again.

"I wouldn't advise this, if I had any other option. The diagnostic team ran through multiple scenarios, and this was the only way we could slow down the cancer!" she interjected.

"Slow down! Slow down! How about that other treatment, Lamolo-" Phon suggested, hesitantly.

"Laminaoma!" Dr. Sommai corrected.

"Yes that! Isn't that supposed to slow down the main cancer. Shouldn't we do that?" he suggested further.

"I am afraid that is no longer an option. With the TSR, we need to be able to access the brain properly for the Neural Transfer," she stopped to catch her breath.

"As I have told you before, Laminaoma creates layers of tumorous cells around the brain, it will no longer be viable for the transfer." she finished.

"Umm –" Phon was out of ideas.

"I know you want to spend more time with her, especially in her current state, but this is a permanent cure we are talking about. Any missteps and we could end up back where we started, only this time we will be out of options!" Dr. Sommai explained sternly.

"Do it!" Phon acquiesced.

Two days later as Siri watched a gossip news report about Sai Lee's latest project in which he plays a handsome Scientist, Dr. Sommai came in with a small syringe in her pocket and sat down next to her. She opened the top and injected it into her IV line. Phon gulped as Siri slowly closed her eyes and her neck sank into the pillow.

Phon's daughter, as he had known her for the past ten years, was now gone.

* * *

Saiman Lin Jian, professionally known as Sai Lee, burst onto the world stage with his boyband — Heartbreakers in October of 2109. After a brief stint and a couple of hundred tours, the band broke up as everyone went their separate ways.

Most of the members faded from the limelight, but not Sai Lee, who reinvented himself into a successful actor as his debut movie Airmen dropped in the Summer of 2117. He played the role of Fighter Pilot who crash landed on a remote island during the South Sea War.

Suffice it to say Airmen was an instant hit as Lee became a global phenomenon, yet again. A new era of star focused filmmaking began as Lee starred, produced and directed 17 more movies, all of which went on to make trillions of dollars on the box office.

After Airmen Sai Lee made a promise to his fans that he will end his filmmaking career once he has done his 19th movie, which symbolized the age at which he became famous with the Heartbreakers.

His rugged looks and a distinct scar that ran from his forehead, across his eye and onto the left side of his face, made him magnetic as stories swirled around social media about how he got the scar. Some said the scar was a result of a fishing trip gone wrong, where the hook dragged across his face when one of his friends cast the line carelessly. Other stories were more fantastical which ranged from him rescuing a kitten from a pack of rabid dogs to him being a Secret Agent who was pretending to be an actor in real life. The truth of the matter was that he sustained the injury during a nasty fall from stage during one of his boy-band tours. Regardless it only added to his legend and solidified his dominance of the New Century Pop Culture.

Mr. Chayaphon Pugkhem spent the last 15 days binge watching those 18 movies of Sai Lee. He knew how much his daughter, (who was now on her 20th day of chemically induced coma) liked Sai Lee. He wanted to share her daughter's life as he completed the last movie titled 'Partners', a buddy cop movie that ended with Sai Lee taking down an international drug organization with his trusty partner and sidekick Lola. The only twist was that Lola was not real, and his romance with her was just a figment of his drug addled mind.

He looked at Siri as the credits rolled and the phone rang. Phon looked away and picked up the phone.

"Mr. Pugkhem! Can you please come to my office, it's quite urgent!" Dr. Sommai's voice blared through the phone.

"What happened Doctor?" Phon asked.

"Just come to my office! It's an emergency!" she seemed panicked as she dropped the call.

Phon was confused. Siri was lying in front of him, her skin a shade of purple from the cryoblue pumping through her veins and her eyes depressed deep into their sockets as she lost more and more weight every week. Why was Dr. Sommai calling him to her office. What could it be?

Ten minutes later, Phon was standing in front of Dr. Sommai's office on the fourth floor. She popped out and looked down the hallway. There were some patients waiting for their outpatient consultation in front of her office.

"Mr. Pugkhem, please come in!" Dr. Sommai invited Phon.

"But he just got here!" one of the outpatients got up, with his file in hand. Dr. Sommai ignored him and pulled Phon into her office.

"What's going on, doctor?" Phon asked as he looked around her office for other people. There was no one, it was just him and Dr. Sommai.

"I have some uh —" Dr. Sommai hesitated as she paced back and forth from her desk to the examination table. Phon remained silent, as he waited for her to finish. She looked flustered and panicked. The dark circles beneath her eyes suggested that she hadn't had a good night's sleep for a while. Whatever she was about to say was definitely bothering her for a while.

"The Total Somatic Replacement – uh – the TSR! we cannot do it anymore!" she said, with the same hesitation.

"What? Why?" Phon asked with justified panic in his voice.

"Umm, it's just that we don't have the replacement body anymore!" she answered, as she looked down in remorse.

"Don't have the body? What do you mean you don't have the body?" he asked, as his voice level rose with the last question.

"It's just that there was an emergency in this other case, which shot to the top of the transplant list, and they had to give the body to —" she tried to explain but was rudely interrupted.

"Shot to the top of the transplant list? how can someone go over a 10-year-old girl with terminal cancer?" Phon roared as he struggled with Dr. Sommai's justification.

"There were some strings pulled at the last moment, and the body was given away. I tried really hard to argue the case with the board but —" she got interrupted again.

"But what? Take me to the board, I will sue each and every one of them if they do the transplant for someone else!" Phon pointed at the door.

"You don't understand, Mr. Pugkhem!" she hesitated.

"The transplant is already complete!" she said in a low voice.

"Already complete? But you can't do this, she doesn't have —" he collapsed on the floor as his back slid against the wall.

"We need help here!" Dr. Sommai yelled into the intercom as four nurses rushed in to help Phon, who now lay unconscious on the floor of Dr. Sommai's office.

* * *

Phon opened his eyes and looked to his left. His daughter Siri was still asleep. The blue face and green veins indicated that she was still in the Cryoblue Coma. Tears streamed down his face as the reality of what just happened dawned on him. His daughter's replacement body had been stolen and the cancer that ravaged her body is now going to finally kill her. He tried to pull his hands from his side to wipe his tears, but he realized he wasn't able to.

"We had to handcuff you to the bed, the Dean of Medicine thinks you are a threat, considering —" Dr. Sommai entered the room as she explained the shackles that now restrained Phon.

"What? Is she still asleep?" Phon stuttered as he wiped his tears on the pillow by turning his head sideways.

"She is still in the coma!" Dr. Sommai confirmed Phon's suspicions.

"The transplant? Is there –" Phon asked as he tried to pull himself up on his bed but then slid back down due to the restraints.

"The sourcing of organs and the prep, takes time, which Siri doesn't have " Dr. Sommai shook her head as she looked back at Siri. Phon's heart sank once again.

"I am here to pull her out of the coma!" she declared as she opened the drawer and pulled out a couple of fresh syringes.

"But the coma, is slowing down the cancer, right?" Phon protested as he turned sideways to look at the doctor who was now filling the syringes with a clear solution.

"If we wait any longer, she might never wake up, even if we are able to find a body for her," she said, as she pushed her tablet in Phon's direction. Phon looked at it with confusion.

"I am going to need your consent to wake her up!" she said as she pushed the tablet some more.

"No! We have to wait!" he turned away looking at the couch that he used to work on, for the past month as Siri's diagnosis came into view.

"Mr. Pugkhem, this is a chance for you to say goodbye. If you don't take it —" she stopped to cough. Phon looked back to see the young doctor swallow a knot. They were in the same boat. She was feeling sad for Siri too. He looked around some more, hoping someone would just bust into the room, informing Dr. Sommai that a new body had been found for the TSR. The doors however, remained predictably closed.

"She is going to wake up?" Phon asked in a low voice.

"Yes!" Dr. Sommai nodded with a tearful smile.

Phon signed the consent form as Dr. Sommai turned towards Siri. She looked at her vitals for a while and then injected the syringe into her IV. Nothing happened as the confused doctor kept staring at the health monitor. Phon looked at her with hope, but she kept checking Siri's pulse with an expression of panic. Something was wrong, Phon felt it.

"Páa!" a broken voice emanated from behind the white coat of Dr. Sommai.

"Siri! I am here!" Phon jumped as the restraints pulled him back down.

"Nurse!" Dr. Sommai yelled as she gave way for Phon to look at Siri. She was still blue, and her mouth only opened to a certain extent. Her face remained expressionless, as she managed to lift up her head from the pillow.

"Take off his restraints!" Dr. Sommai ordered the Nurse.

"But the Dean, she uh –" the Nurse hesitated.

"I will talk to the Dean!" Dr. Sommai roared as the Nurse jumped in place and rushed to Phon's bedside. She pushed in a code into the panel at the base of the bed and the shackles came loose. Phon jumped up from his bed as IV lines broke off from his arm. He hugged her daughter hard and picked her up from the bed as the wires that protruded from her became taut.

"When will we —cough– go home, Páa?" Siri asked in her broken voice.

"Soon!" Phon pulled away from the hug and looked at his daughter whose eyes were now becoming droopy. An alarm from the health monitors prompted Dr. Sommai to pull Siri away from Phon as she checked her neck for a pulse.

"Code blue!" Dr. Sommai yelled as the nurse in the room jumped to her side and called the phone mounted to the wall next to Siri's bed. Two other doctors rushed into the room as a second nurse pulled Phon away.

"O2 sats are at 78, Intubating now!" a doctor yelled from the side where Phon was standing.

"Hyperventilate to bring down the ICP. Push mannitol — 100 grams" Dr. Sommai ordered the other doctor as the first one pushed a tube down Siri's throat.

"Mannitol going in. Vitals are unstable — BP's 190/100, heart rate 40." the Doctor yelled back as Dr. Sommai rushed to the other side.

"Prepare for compressions, if the heart stops!" Dr. Sommai bellowed as Phon crashed into the glass door as he stepped back.

"Get him out of here!" the younger doctor ordered the nurse.

"No! let him stay!" Dr. Sommai stopped the nurse as Phon stepped closer to the bed.

"Flatline detected!" the younger doctor pulled away from the blatant overruling of his instruction to report the ringing sound that now emanated from the health monitor.

"Start compressions! Give me a milligram of epinephrine, IV push!" Dr. Sommai ordered the nurse.

"Epi's in. No response. Still no rhythm," the nurse reported.

"Push another epi. Prepare the defibrillator," Dr. Sommai instructed once more as a nurse pulled out the defibrillator pads and handed them to the doctor.

"Charging to 200, clear!" Dr. Sommai roared as the two doctors and a nurse stepped away from Siri. Siri's back arced as the paddles hit her chest.

"No pulse. No change on the monitor!" the Nurse reported.

"One more round of compressions!" Dr. Sommai yelled again as she climbed on top of the bed to push against Siri's chest. Phon slid against the glass wall, as teardrops stained his green hospital gown.

Twenty minutes went by as the sound of the defibrillator charging and Dr. Sommai's orders echoed in the room. Phon was now sitting on the floor, looking at the flashes of doctors passing him by.

"She's gone. Call it!" a younger doctor announced as he stepped back.

"Time of death 3:47 AM!" Dr. Sommai announced, stepping back as Phon snapped back from his daze.

Siri was finally gone!

* * *

"Sorry for the inconvenience but I can't come to the phone right now, please leave a message." a cheerful voice of Phon's answering machine greeted an incoming call that had been ringing for a while.

"Mr. Pugkhem, I have emailed you the documents that you requested," Patty's voice emanated from the answering machine, in Phon's study.

"I know you are not available, but Mr. Santino was asking about you. He wants to know when you will be back?" Patty spoke as Phon stirred up from his nap, in the home office chair.

He heaved forward to open his laptop and stirred up a dust storm, from the inch thick dirt that had gathered on his study table. He opened his email and started going through the documents that Patty had just sent.

"I will inform him that you will not be back for the week. On a personal note, I hope you —" Patty was interrupted as Phon picked up the phone.

"I am coming in today; can you pull the consultants from the filming division and check if anyone is working on Saiman Lee's latest project?" Phon ordered his assistant as he looked at the medical documents that Patty had procured from a high-profile cosmetic clinic in the Northeastern Territories.

"I can check but —" Patty began but was once again interrupted by Phon.

"Just do it!" Phon barked as he dropped the call and zoomed into one of the inset images in the document.

The medical records from Katerina Aesthetic Clinic in Busan were that of a patient codenamed — Subject 06011995.

The patient had undergone an emergency Total Somatic Replacement as a replacement body was procured from the Southeast Eurasian Territories. Initially intended to be a female, the specimen was further reconstructed for a male body replacement. The distinguishing feature for Post Replacement Identification process or PRI as the bold heading atop page number 8 read, was a scar that ran from the forehead, across the eye and to the left of his face.

* * *

Phon vomited over the portside of the Heartbreaker as an Island with Limestone Karsts defenses rose dramatically out of the water, came into view.

"Would you like some more seasickness pills, Mr. Pugkhem?" Kom asked Phon.

Kom, more formally known as Komkrit Warikorn, was the VP of Creative and Technical Consulting at SCG. He was accompanying Phon to the Arronax Islands where the shooting for Saiman Lee's latest untitled project was underway.

"No! I am fine," Phon refused the pills as he knew the vomitting was not seasickness. He cleaned his mouth with a small paper napkin, enthusiastically offered by Kom and headed back inside.

"As I was saying, Mr. Lee was so happy that you had reached out, he offered his own personal yacht — The Heartbreaker, to bring you to the islands!" Kom gestured towards the captain's chair which was more ceremonial than useful, since the Yacht moved autonomously.

"Did he say anything else?" Phon asked hoping that Lee knew him from somewhere else. The obvious suspicion that plagued Phon's mind, ever since Lee invited him to the islands, was that the actor was aware that he stole the replacement body from him and his daughter.

"He just said that 'he is a fan of your work!'" Kom informed him as he accepted a champagne glass from a stewardess.

Phon was confused. How can an internationally acclaimed actor be a fan of a corporate Lawyer? This thought soon purged from his mind as the Arronax Island Pier finally appeared on the horizon. It was bizarre, to say the least.

"What is that?" Phon asked as he looked at the Pier building through which a huge rock popped out, not as something which destroyed the building but as something which was part of the wooden building to begin with.

"I can tell you, but it's better if you hear it from the man himself!" Kom smiled as he signaled Phon to move to the front of the Yacht for disembarking. As he stepped out on the wobbly floating Pier, he looked around, to find more abnormalities. The limestone karsts had huge holes in them, which made them look like they survived a bombing raid. The road that connected the pier with the inner island had a huge tree in the middle of it. Phon pinched himself to make sure he wasn't dreaming his revenge upon Sai Lee, like he had been doing for the past weeks.

He walked slowly towards the weird pier building with its many ticket counters that gave access to the disjointed road that lead into the Island. The rock formation became clear as Phon realized there was moss formation on the its surface.

"Welcome to Arronax Island, Mr. Warikorn and you must be Mr. Pukhem!" a beautiful girl in a loose sundress welcomed the two overdressed gentlemen as she struggled to pronounce Phon's name.

"Jackie, how are you?" Kom stumbled forward and hugged the beautiful girl. As he pulled out from the hug, he planted a drunken kiss on her lips. Phon looked on in shock, having realized that Kom was a married man.

"I am good, Mr. Warikorn, this way please!" she gestured towards an open top SUV that was parked at the end of the pier. Phon smiled forcefully as he started walking towards the SUV. He could have sworn Jackie wiped her lips as soon as Kom turned towards the vehicle.

Moments later they were swerving through the tarmac road covered with lush green forests on both sides. He looked around to see small clearings in the forest where sunlight fell to reveal something that glowed bright red. Phon wiped his eyes as he looked inside the vehicle. Kom was sitting to his left as he ogled Jackie's legs, who sat in the front passenger seat.

"Mr. Lee bought this island, a decade ago, to film his last project!" Jackie informed as she pulled the hem of her dress to cover her knees.

"That kid has quite the foresight!" Kom remarked as Jackie glowered at him. Phon knew he had crossed a line. Nobody likes their boss to be referred to as a 'kid'.

"What? He is a kid again, isn't he?" Kom joked as Jackie spun around in what was clearly disgustful anger.

"This is it!" Phon thought to himself. This crucial piece of information has confirmed his suspicion that Saiman Lee is the one who stole his daughter's replacement body.

"We are here!" Jackie announced as the doors to the SUV flew open and Phon stepped out.

At the end of the road was a small seafront house, which from the looks off it was a little too much into the sea as waves crashed against its front and bubbled to the side.

A man stood on the balcony that curved out from the right side of the house. He was looking out into the horizon as the closing doors of the vehicle made him turn back.

"Welcome my friends to the set of Last Thursday!" a younger Saiman Lee welcomed the two gentlemen from Siam Consulting Group into his house.

* * *

"What is Last Thursday, if you don't mind me asking?" Phon spoke up as Kom who was still busy chatting up Jackie.

"Last Thursday!" Lee paused as he turned around to look at Phon.

"— is going to be my magnum opus!" he declared as he opened his arms wide and welcomed his two guests into his humble abode. From the looks of it was anything but humble. The walls were lined with supersized moving posters of his movies and in the middle of it all stood a life-size statue of Saiman as he sang into a golden mic.

"I meant —" Phon stuttered as he looked into the face of Lee. He looked younger and resembled his likeness to the Heartbreaker boyband days. He definitely had the TSR, most probably with the body that was meant for Siri. His stomach sank as thoughts of Siri's last moments flooded his mind. Reality crashed upon him as the waves did against the house, he would never be able to talk to his daughter again.

"Please have a seat, Mr. Pugkhem!" Lee gestured towards the ornate couch in the middle of his living room as Phon realized how Lee was able to pronounce his surname with perfection.

"I would rather stand!" Phon declined as his blood curdled by the looks of the smooth skin that Lee now wore.

"Forgive me but I think I sense some hostility from you!" Lee remarked as Kom pulled away from Jackie.

"Oh no! no! Mr. Lee!" Kom began his introductions having realized he had flirted long enough and the temperature in the room just rose.

"Mr. Pugkhem just meant —" Kom was interrupted by Lee.

"Don't like us creative types, do you Mr. Pugkhem?" he said with a smile as the tension eased.

"Yeah!" Kom let out a sycophantic smile as he looked at Lee.

"Jackie, why don't you take Mr. Warikorn here, to our production setup for the climax scene, maybe get his opinion on the financials as well" Lee dismissed the annoying Kom, who at first looked taken aback but then smiled at the thought of spending the evening with Jackie.

"Now! Mr. Pugkhem, I see you have been a curious man!" Lee sat down on the opposing couch as he picked up a small bottle containing a viscous green fluid.

"Well, you don't look like a man at all, it seems that you have time-travelled back to your teenage years!" Phon mocked, unsure of what he was going to do next.

"Oh this! Yeah, just underwent a highly risky procedure to finish off the film!" Lee looked at himself and sipped the green fluid.

Phon straightened up. His jaw wide open, at the thought. The superstar actor that sat infront of him had underwent the TSR, for a film. It wasn't some health emergency, neither was it something terminal. The man that sat in front him took his daughters life to satisfy his artistic ambitions.

"A film!" Phon mumbled to himself as his blood boiled over.

"Yes! A film, and not just any film, my final film!" Lee began his gloating as he got up and walked into the dark door which was the only way out of the living room except the entrance. Phon looked around for something sharp, but other than a small plasma guitar that hung around the statue of Sai Lee, there was nothing deadly in the room.

"What are you waiting for? Follow me!" Lee peeked from the dark room as he signaled Phon to follow him.

Phon obliged, hoping to find a potential murder weapon in the next room. He followed him inside to find that it wasn't a room, but a stairway that descended into the beach house. He carefully stepped on the first steps as he saw Lee disappear at the bottom. A deafening crash made him jump and almost trip his way down the stairs.

"It's just my meditation room! Don't mind the waves, Mr. Pugkhem" Lee pointed towards thick glass wall against which the waves from the oceans crashed in succession. About a quarter of the wall was underwater as it showed the water rescind back for a moment, only to hit the wall with another crash a moment later.

"Mr. Pugkhem, sounds very professional, may I call you something else?" Lee looked back to see the cold expressions on Phon's face.

"Sure!" Phon agreed reluctantly.

"Khem! I shall call you Khem! How does it sound?" Lee said playfully. Phon nodded.

"One more floor, Khem!" Lee announced, as they kept descending further and further. Phon didn't like his new nickname, but he was here to kill Lee, not discuss informality with his daughter's killer.

A morbid thought crossed Phon's mind. Was Lee already aware that Phon was here to kill him? Is he going to strike first?

"Focus!" snapped Phon.

"Huh! Did you say something?" Lee asked as his voice echoed against the basement walls. Wherever they were going, it was well below sea level.

At last the stairs ended and a shiny bunker door came into view. Lee walked towards the panel and pressed his finger on the biometric sensor. It flashed red.

"Oh sorry! Ever since the replacement nothing works!" Lee said, as he let out a mild chuckle.

He pulled out the number pad and entered a very long passcode. The panel flashed green and the shiny aluminum (at least Phon thought it was aluminum) slid open.

"Welcome to my Mind Palace!" Lee announced as the lights whirred back on, the door behind them closed and the sound of the waves receded into distance.

* * *

"The idea for Last Thursday struck me as I was driving back from my parent's house!" Lee began his explanation as the room fell dark and a picture of a small cottage appeared on the left wall. The whole room was a visual space, it followed Lee's every word.

"My mother has just been diagnosed with terminal cancer!" Lee continued as a photo of an elderly woman, jam packed with tubes appeared on the right wall. It reminded Phon of Siri, and for a moment his anger subsided as he followed Lee's story, which started mirroring a little bit of his own.

"At that moment, I just wanted things to go back the way they were last week!" he swallowed a knot and a picture of Heartbreakers in their teenage years appeared on the front wall. They were practicing in a garage as Lee held a plasma guitar and stood in front of the mic. They looked weird, this was definitely before they became famous.

"That's when it struck me, what if I could take a snapshot of the world and can recreate it the same way at any point of time!" Lee turned around as the walls went dark again.

Phon understood Lee in that moment. If there was a way he could go back in time, when Siri was healthy, and played around like a normal child, he would quit his job and spend each waking moment with her. Another wave of remorse washed over him as the walls turned white.

"I knew I could never do that in reality, but as you are well aware Khem, that all science needs is a bit of imagination!" Lee turned around as another image formed behind Phon. A tablet with a dark cover and luminous green group of jellyfish huddled closely. In the same luminous green and ornate writing, it said — Twenty Thousand Leagues Under the Seas.

"That my friend is a book, a novel to be more exact, written by a visionary writer named Jules Verne, around 300 years ago!" Lee explained as Phon walked closer to examine the unmoving image of this so-called novel.

"He dreamed of an underwater world explored by an underwater vehicle, called Nautilus commanded by a mysterious character, who is simply known as Captain Nemo." he began explaining the story, stored within this novel.

"The Nautilus is chased around the seas by a ragtag group of explorers amongst which is an Ichthyologist named Professor Pierre Arronax," he stopped to let me take in the context, as the Pier with Rock Building appeared in front of me.

"The name of this Island!" Phon exclaimed.

"Exactly! I renamed the island from Panek Island to Arronax Island, after the most curious of the characters from the novel" he smiled to appreciate the fact that Phon could keep up.

"The tragedy was that they used the concept of Nautilus to design the Submarines, which were used profusely in the first and second World War, to sink ships!" Lee explained as another image formed of a black tower peeking from the water surface as a ship moved in the distance.

"Regardless! My point is, if we dream it, they will make it!" Lee declared as the room went dark again.

"30 years ago, when I left my band and started making movies, I decided that I would make only 19, one for every year I had spent with my mother!" Lee said, in a low voice. Phon had remained silent until now. He waited for Lee to continue.

"Last Thursday explores a physicist's journey as he detects a dark matter storm that will ravage multiple worlds including Earth." Lee began again as a small image of Earth formed behind him and a larger darker abyss enveloped it.

"He creates a snapshot of civilization, only to be restored from, a million years later, when the storm has passed and Earth is habitable again!" Another image formed of Earth undergoing metamorphosis from blue, to black, then red and finally blue again.

"But!" Lee stopped as the visual space descended into darkness yet again.

"There is something wrong with the snapshot! Things aren't exactly the way they were before!" the screens erupted into bizarre images, much like the Pier building that Phon saw when he entered the island. There were redwood trees growing out of the ocean, deserts were flooding with tsunamis and finally there were open cavities in the Earth which bared glowing red embers. Phon realized that this was the glow that he saw when they were passing the lush forests.

"The physicist's job is to find his younger self and fix the snapshot so that the younger self can try again!" Lee concluded as the screens became a comfortable amber glow to light the room they were in.

"But what happens to the older version of the physicist?" Phon's curiosity finally gave in as another smile appeared on Lee's face.

"You have to watch the movie to find out!" Lee joked as Phon stepped back. Similar to the room upstairs, this room was even more devoid of lethal objects. Just four visual walls and mild sounds of the waves crashing above.

"Why did you send the yacht?" Phon mumbled as Lee stepped closer to hear what the old lawyer was saying.

"Ah! That's because I am a fan of your work!" Lee repeated Kom's words.

"What do you mean?" Phon asked, now realizing in the warm glow of amber, how perfect Lee's new skin looked.

"I intend to donate all of my wealth to cancer research after my final movie and for that I need a Conservator. Someone who understands corporate and tax law, to make sure the money is used effectively, and the government cannot get it's grubby hands on it!" Lee explained as the door slid back open and they stepped out. Phon's anger subsided once again as he now weighed his choice for revenge against the opportunity of using the enormous wealth of Sai Lee that could help millions like him evade the misery that he had to endure.

"Why —uh — me?" Phon stuttered as they climbed up the stairs.

"Well there are two reasons!" Lee replied as they entered the meditation room, which vibrated with the crashing waves of the tumultuous sea.

"And they are!" Phon egged him on.

"The first one is Arapaima vs Jerome Pearson!" Lee spoke as a wave crashed against the front glass wall.

Arapaima vs Jerome Pearson was a case that Phon took on his younger years. He successfully argued in International Court of Justice that Arapaima which was a Syntel or Synthetic Intelligence deserved the same rights as a sentient being and hence the fatal attack by the domestic terrorist Jerome Pearson, on the data center that housed Arapaima, should be considered as intentional premeditated murder.

Because of this landmark judgement all Syntels whether they owned and controlled large megacorporation or worked in the local repair shop to mend workstations, were given equal standing against humans.

"Oh!" Phon reminisced as a weak smile appeared on his face.

"The second reason is your daughter!" Lee concluded as he turned around and walked towards the stairs.

Another wave crashed against the glass wall as Phon stood in the meditation room, unable to move in either direction.

* * *

There was a knock on the door as Phon woke up in the deluxe suite of Panek Talay, a seven-star hotel on the other side of Arronax Island.

"Mr. Lee has invited you to the after party aboard his yacht," the hotel bellhop peeked inside as he gave a small tableaf to Phon.

"What afterparty?" Phon inquired.

"Well they wrapped up the production on the movie last night, so uh —" the bellhop answered.

"When is it?" Phon interrupted.

"In an hour sir! The Heartbreaker yacht will leave the pier at 1230" bellhop answered again.

"Understood!" Phon proceeded to close the door in his face, but the bellhop stopped the door halfway.

"Should I ready a car, to take you to the pier, Sir? Mr. Lee specifically requested your presence!" the bellhop insisted.

"Uh ycah surc!" rcspondcd Phon as hc slammcd thc door, with extra force into the bellhop's face.

An hour later, Phon was walking out of the lobby towards the waiting car. He was unable to get much sleep due to the explosions in the distance, which he now knew were set pieces for the production of Last Thursday.

After months of work, he had tracked down his daughter's body thief. But now that same thief offered something larger. A chance at his own redemption and Phon's redemption as he looked back at years of neglect towards his own daughter.

If he decides to go through with this new job offer and becomes the Conservator for trillions of dollars in wealth, aimed towards cancer research, he could finally honor Siri's memory.

On the other hand, the last statement from Lee spoke did rub him the wrong way. He did not know whether Lee was mocking him for having stolen the body away or was he using his daughter's cancer as a matter of fact to guilt him into the Conservator's job.

"We are here!" the autonomic system on the car announced as Phon saw the mega yacht parked near the Pier. The word Heartbreaker was emblazoned on the back as a gaggle of beautiful bikini clad women danced in the jacuzzi on the top deck.

Phon sighed as he stepped out of the car and made his way down to the jetty. He did not know what he was doing, all he knew was that he wanted to know more. The most important question in his mind was — Did Lee know that he was taking the body away from Siri?

"Khem! I am glad you could make it," a smiling Saiman Lee welcomed him aboard.

"Your friend is already here!" he pointed towards Kom who was dancing in his trunks, surrounded by multiple women. Phon let out another sigh as he stepped onto the yacht.

"Did you get a chance to think about my proposal?" Lee asked in whispers as people rushed around him to the back of the yacht to say goodbye to the island staff.

"I will do it!" Phon responded as a smile spread across Lee's face. He shook Phon's hand vigorously and then made his way to the top deck.

"Ladies and Gentlemen, my filmmaking career as you know is finally over!" he declared as every face on the yacht turned towards him.

"I am going out the same way I came in, young and on top!" he pumped his fist as applause broke out across the yacht. Phon stepped back a little.

"As most of you know I recently underwent a highly risky procedure to get this new body, which is exactly as old as the first day I stepped into a film studio!" Lee announced as everyone whispered amongst themselves. Apparently only some of the people were aware of this drastic reversal of age in their primary thespian.

"And after weeks of ingesting this green piss," he pointed to a small cylindrical container, that said 'IMMUNOLESS, BATCH 345'.

"I can finally drink again!" he picked up a large champagne bottle and blew the cork into the sea as he poured it all over the ladies in the jacuzzi.

"And finally, the best for last, Mr. Pugkhem here, the greatest lawyer of our generation has agreed to join me as my Conservator as I finally enjoy my retirement!" Lee grabbed Phon by the shoulder and pulled him closer for all to see.

"Let's fucking party!" he announced as the yacht broke out in a mix of applause and hooting. Phon moved towards the captain's chair to let the rest of them enjoy this moment. He saw

Lee take off his shirt, multiple faded surgical scars ran down his back.

"I AM NEVER GONNA DIE!" he roared as he jumped into the ocean from the top deck.

Phon felt lightheaded as he questioned his most recent choice to join Lee. From the back of the yacht a completely drenched and hammered Lee emerged to accost Phon once more.

"Jackie why don't you take my friend Khem here and introduce him to our lady friends who seem to be enjoying the sun!" Lee ordered Jackie as Phon remained entrenched in distressing thought.

"Why? You are not a family man, are you? Come on, enjoy yourself!" Lee nudged Phon towards Jackie.

"Did you know?" Phon mumbled under his breath.

"Huh did you say something?" Lee asked over the loud music.

"Did you know, about the body?" he asked clearly.

"What body?" Lee answered, with a confused expression on his face as he sat down on the dining table adorned with various fruits and cheese platters.

"The body that you took, did you know who it belonged to?" Phon roared as Lee leaned his head back.

"This body!" he asked as he pointed towards his scar ridden torso.

"Did you know who you took it from?" Phon asked as he neared the table.

"Some local girl, they didn't tell me much!" Lee answered as he ate a slice of pineapple.

It all happened in an instant, as Phon picked up the knife from the cheese plate and thrust it into Saiman Lee's chest.

A blood-curdling scream from Jackie, made everyone turn towards the center of the Yacht where Saiman Lee, twitched in his own pool of blood. Above him stood the hotshot lawyer who was just assigned the Conservator to Lee's entire estate.

***

"Checking in, this is the Chief of Staff from the Mayoral Office of Baiplew for Mr. Pugkhem" a voice blared on the answering machine as Phon jumped up to pick up the phone in his study.

"This is Mr. Pugkhem," he answered the Chief of Staff.

"Mr. Pugkhem, my name is Bethany, I am calling to confirm an in-person appointment with the mayor at 2 PM today," she said in her robotic monotonous voice.

"Confirmed" replied Phon as he pulled up his tablet and pressed the button to call the caretaker.

"Yes Mr. Pukem!" Lisa, the temporary caretaker who still couldn't pronounce his name properly, entered the study.

"Lisa, can you please tidy up the apartment, we are expecting some company today," the raspy voice of Phon gave out as he coughed a little.

"And would you mind calling my parole officer that I might be required to step out of the house, to greet the mayor!" Phon added as Lisa doubled back for the second instruction.

It had been fifteen long years since that fateful sunny day aboard the Heartbreaker Yacht. Mr. Chayaphon Pugkhem was immediately arrested by the authorities as the yacht came into port. He was later flown out to Baiplew where he pleaded to the manslaughter of famous actor Saiman Lee. He served 14 long years in the Continental Prison and was now out on parole, doing some legal consulting work for his old firm, SCG.

He received a peculiar call from his former boss and current client Mr. Santino, that the mayor and his trust want to enlist his services and have requested to meet him at the earliest possible opportunity. Owing to the fact that Phon was still on house arrest, the mayor had graciously agreed to meet him at his apartment. The clock struck 2, as Phon instructed Lisa to be on the lookout for government cars.

There was a soft knock on the door as Lisa rushed to open it. The smiling face of Mayor greeted the young caretaker, behind which Phon stood smiling ready to welcome his guest.

"Mr. Mayor! Welcome!" Phon widened his smile some more to invite the stout mayor inside his apartment.

"Please call me, Madiq!" the short stout Mayor smiled and entered the apartment as two of his security details remained posted outside.

"I think I will be fine, George, thanks!" Mayor Madiq ordered the third guard to stand down as he followed him inside the apartment.

"Let's talk in my study!" Phon gestured the mayor towards his workspace.

"They say you are the best!" The mayor walked into the study as he walked towards the window to look at the street downstairs.

"Probably an overstatement" Phon let out a weak smile as the mayor walked around his study.

"How can I help you, Mr. Mayor –uh– Madiq" Phon asked hesitantly.

"You see, I have a problem with my trust, the money inside it belonged to someone else, and I have no way of recovering it without the authorization of the original owner!" Madiq jumped straight to the point.

"How can the trust be yours and the money be someone else's?" Phon asked as he signaled Lisa to bring in some tea.

"The money belonged to a friend of mine, he is, let's say for the purpose of our conversation, uh deceased!" Madiq smiled as he looked away from the left window.

"Some tea, Mr. Mayor or buttered toast perhaps!" Phon offered to which the mayor shook his head.

"Did you say the friend who deposited money into your trust, is dead?" Phon looked up unable to grasp the peculiar situation.

"Murdered, to be more precise, but dead either way yes!" Madiq answered.

"Off the record, did you have anything to do with his murder?" Phon answered as a sincere expression dawned on the mayor's face.

"I might have been involved, unknowingly of course," Madiq's expression turned sincere.

"How can you murder someone, unknowingly?" Phon asked as a chill descended down his spine.

"If I am not mistaken, didn't you go to jail for murder?" the mayor changed topics as the spoon fell from Phon's hand.

"I beg your pardon, Mr. Mayor, but that is not relevant in this case" Phon let out another weak smile.

"Oh! But it is," Madiq responded with his own smile, more sinister and less weak. Phon stepped back, his heart racing.

"Why did you kill that poor actor?" the short and stout Mayor asked as he slid his hand in his coat pocket.

"Mr. Mayor, I think we are getting off topic —" Phon hesitated some more.

"Why did you kill him, Khem?" the mayor pushed deep into his pocket as Phon tightened his grip around the butter knife.

CHAPTER 6

EIDOLONS

"Please state your name for this confirmation hearing" Congressman McArthur asked in a soft voice.

"My name is Lieutenant Simeon Freeman, 5th Special Forces Group, Airborne, Retired!" I formally introduced myself.

"What are your personal opinions on the Moo Baan Suay Massacre, Lieutenant Freeman?" Congresswoman Quintero asked smugly as she looked down at me.

"Alleged Massacre!" boomed Congressman McArthur.

"Yes! Alleged Massacre? Do you think it was justified, given the state of things?" Quintero rephrased her question with a forced smile.

"I feel it's —uh– excuse me!" I coughed and reached for some water as the entire semi-circle of vain politicians waited for my answer.

"I believe," I adjusted my throat "that there was definite misuse of power and systemic abuse of authority during the aftermath of Wan Offensive!" I answered as I put down the glass of water.

I can't believe they are interviewing me in a public hearing. I thought it was just going to be some old army geezers and suspicious looking men in black suits, but I guess when your government has fumbled this bad, they have to do everything in public to cover their ass. If it means having open hearings, to select the security detail for the 'Most Hated Man in America', then so be it.

Welcome to the worst job interview of all time!

"What are your feelings towards Private Miller?" Quintero stopped to look at McArthur, "about his 'alleged' treason charges?" Quintero asked another question, with a heavy emphasis on the word 'alleged' as she leaned forwards to raise her eyebrows at McArthur.

"I believe Private Miller, acted according to his belief systems!" I answered quickly. I had to keep these things short and to the point. The more I spoke, the more pouncy these fucking jackals might get.

"What do you mean, his belief systems? Do you not believe Mr. Miller had a human responsibility to report this genocide, at the hands of the US military?" Quintero pounced. Shit!

"Alleged 'Genocide'" interrupted McArthur.

"Yes! Yes! alleged 'genocide'" agreed Quintero as she looked back at me.

"I meant I am —" I stuttered.

"I know exactly what you mean!" Her eyes lit up like a hyena in the dark.

"I believe his right —" I went back to the beginning, but it was too late.

"I know exactly what you believe, you think his belief systems have made him a traitor to this country, don't you Lieutenant Freeman?" Quintero suggested. The bitch might just fall off, if she leaned any further off of her high table.

"Jesus! Quintero, let the man speak!" Congressman Valerio jumped in, with a nasty expression on his face. Quintero shot a disgusted look at him and leaned back. I adjusted my tie.

"I believe Mr. Miller was practicing his First Amendment Right and I wish to defend his use of such right, as given to him by the United States Constitution!" I announced to the room as it fell silent except for the camera flashes and a couple of coughs.

Quintero glowered at me with the same disgust that she reserved for Valerio earlier. McArthur smiled in the corner, while Valerio himself looked indifferent.

"No more questions! We will let you know about our decision!" Quintero declared after some deliberation with the rest of the committee members.

"Thank you for your time!" McArthur beamed at me. The old bastard thinks since I am a retired marine, I will do what needs to be done and get rid of the traitor or at least get out of the way as someone else carries out their patriotic duty and take out this traitor. But I am afraid he is in for a huge surprise.

To be really honest, I think what Private Noah Miller did, by leaking those tapes and transcripts about the Moo Baan Suay Patrol Team, took an immense amount of courage. If Congress approves me for his security detail I will do everything in my power to see that cruel bastard Everett spends the rest of his life in jail for what he did to those poor villagers.

Fuck him and the rest of his Omega company!

* * *

We have broken their defenses, crushed their spirits and vanquished any hopes for independence. Soon, every Kaling will join me in the service of the Greatest of Emperors, Chakravartin Samrat Ashoka.

"I can smell the salt in the air, Ajju!" the Great Emperor declared atop his tall dark horse.

"The sea is not far from here, my lord!" I bowed my head and approached his steed.

"Grandfather would be proud!" his Majesty mumbled to himself as he turned around to see a lone rider emerge from behind the hills.

"What does he want?" the Great Emperor asked calmly.

"Let me handle this, my lord!" I volunteered as I stepped away from my horse and moved in the direction of the approaching rider.

"Nayak Bhagwadajjukam!" the rider yelled out my name as he jumped from the horse before it could come to a stop.

"What is it?" I asked sternly as he caught his breath. I looked back to sneak a look at the Emperor, but he had already turned around to look down at the wide Mahanadi River, which marked the edge of the Mauryan Empire and the start of the Kalinga Rebel Kingdom.

"Message from Tamralipta!" he handed me a palm scroll and stepped back. I unfurled the dried palm leaf, which bore the seal of a fish. It was sent by Biswajit, my spy in the port city of Tamralipta.

My eyes widened as I read one sentence after another. I dismissed the rider and walked back towards the Emperor.

"My lord! We have word from —" I began, but before I could complete.

"Tamralipta!" he completed my sentence, "Padmanabhan is trying to escape!" he said as he turned his horse around.

"Yes my lord! But how do you —" I asked confusedly.

"He mustn't escape!" the Emperor said calmly.

"But my lord, if the Kaling Rebel King runs away, there will be less blood spilled!" I protested and to my surprise, the Emperor let out a graceful smile.

"We have the choice of spilling blood now, so that our descendants can live in peace!" the Great Emperor continued in his calm voice.

"What do you mean, my lord?" a deep shame washed over me as I struggled to grasp the meaning of my lord's wise words.

"If Padmanabhan escapes, Kaling will always be a rebel state to Mauryan rule. They will have hope for the return of their king. Our children will have to deal with the thousand cuts these rebels will inflict upon us. We must kill him, to crush any hopes for an Independent Kalinga!" my lord explained calmly.

"I will send word to my men, immediately." I bowed deeper than before as I saw the feet of his great dark steed shuffle back and forth.

"We must get back to camp, the sun is about to set!" he said as he pointed at the orange sky, bathed in purple hue. I nodded and turned back to climb on my horse. we cantered back to our camp beside the narrowest pass of the turbulent Matron River Mahanadi.

As we approached the camp, I signaled one of the guards to fetch my scribe. The Great Emperor split away towards his own tent, the largest by far in the entire river basin that was littered with Mauryan flags, and slowly igniting fires as dusk turned into night.

"Send word to Biswajit!" I ordered the Scribe as I entered my own tent.

"What do you want me to write, my lord?" the Scribe asked with a bow as I started taking off my breastplate and sword.

"The large ship in the harbor must never begin its journey!" I dictated as the Scribe pulled out his Talapatra (dried palm leaf) and his reed pen.

"Anything else you would like to add, my lord?" the Scribe asked with reverence. I pulled the clasp on my breastplate as it fell down on the ground.

"Nothing else, fetch my signet!" I signaled towards the small chest near my bedding on the ground. The Scribe hobbled towards the chest as his robes caught the bare palm of his feet. I turned towards the Scribe, as I wrapped my hands around the hilt of my sword. In a flash my sword was at the impostor's neck as I kicked him onto my bedspread.

"A Scribe never asks for more!" I put the sword to his neck as he slunk back into the corner.

"Kalinga will always be free!" he bellowed as he pulled up his Rudraksha bead necklace and bit hard on one of the smoother beads. I lurched forwards to prevent him from swallowing the poison, but it was too late. He started frothing at the mouth as the rest of his body went into seizure.

I stepped back as a bead of sweat travelled across my temple and into my eyes.

"I must find the Emperor" a thought ran across my mind.

* * *

"You were in Afghanistan? Weren't you?" the disgraced Private Noah Miller asked in a shaky voice.

"Yes, I was!" I answered as I checked the door handle to his hotel room.

"Did you —uh— see any action?" he asked hesitantly. I turned around to look at the skinny 19-year-old kid, who was sitting on his bed, wearing a dark suit that only enhanced his lanky frame. His face was populated with blistering acne and his tussled brown hair made him look younger than he actually was.

"Yeah! I was in the Special Forces," I answered as I moved towards the wall glass window on the other side of the hotel room "action is just part of the job!"

"Isn't that supposed to be a secret, I mean you shouldn't be able to tell me that you were Special Forces, right?" he stuttered as I felt his stare burn into the side of my face. I looked down into the street where a sea of reporters were reluctantly making way for a large black SUV.

"You should be the last person to talk about secrets!" I turned around and smiled at the young man. He didn't smile back, instead he looked down at his shoe with renewed shame.

Private Noah Miller was born in the Shipshewana Amish Commune outside Highwayton, Indiana to the happily married couple of Samuel and Mary Miller. He knew a simple way of life, where God and community were the two most important things.

At the tender age of 16, Noah, along with five other boys from the commune, ventured out into the modern world as part of their Rumspringa, a tradition where an Amish boy is allowed to explore the outside world and experience everything it has to offer, before finally settling down at home.

After a year, only two boys who ventured out on their Rumspringa, returned to Shipshewana and Noah wasn't one of them. He had taken a lover by the name of Karen Ramonski, a

32-year-old single mother of two, who worked at the local pharmacy.

After months of living with Karen in Westhead RV Park, she realized that Noah didn't have any real-world skills and he was more of a third child to her than a provider. Naturally, she abandoned young Noah as he came home one day to find the trailer park skirting in place of where Karen's trailer used to be.

Filled with rage and heartbreak, Noah ran into an Army Recruiter who promised him purpose and a chance to be a man. Both of which appealed to Noah, since he was in no mood to return to Shipshewana empty handed.

After his training, he was deployed to the ongoing Burmese Conflict in Southeast Asia where he served under Captain Shawn Everett and his Omega Company. Captain Everett, by various accounts, was a raging lunatic with a penchant for violence. He didn't take kindly to Private Miller's meek and non-violent ways. Suffice it to say life got evermore harder for Noah, as time went on.

Among the many militant groups that threatened the stability of the region, a particularly vicious group called the Suvarna Tigers was not happy with the US presence in their country. They made it their mission to push back on US positions, every chance they got. One such chance came in the form of Wan Offensive where the Suvarna Tigers, with the help of the other militant groups blew up an American supply line that was entering the country from the Indian Border. The entire military leadership was shocked at this brazen attempt by a small terrorist group on the mightiest military on Earth. But no retaliation came, as the senior leadership decided to push on in its efforts to install a US friendly government in the capital.

Amongst the various scorned servicemen, none were more unhappy than Captain Everett and his band of zealous Sergeants. Their unhappiness found objective when they received report of a nearby village, who was seen celebrating and helping the Suvarna Tigers. Everett convened his company which included the young Private Noah Miller. Unbeknownst to his senior leadership, the Omega company descended upon the allegedly rebel friendly village of Moo Ban Suay.

What happened next, shocked young Noah to the core, as the soldiers dragged and killed most of the men, who were returning from a long day at the farm. Some soldiers maimed the teenagers who protested Everett's cruelty. Many more unspeakable atrocities happened that day as Private Noah Miller stood by and watched.

The next day, the news of these atrocities reached the high command, who immediately put Everett on paid leave and ordered a classified inquiry into the matter. A small platoon was sent into the village to gather photographs and accounts from the villagers. They were also given certain allowances to help convince the villagers to keep this under wraps. When they returned, the photographs and other media were uploaded to an air-gapped server awaiting a full review.

That same night, Private Noah sneaked into the server room and copied all the files from the server and applied for furlough the very next day. Upon returning stateside, he reached out to a small newspaper in his hometown of Highwayton Indiana, by the name Highway Herald.

It mostly provided news to the Amish communities in the form of basic newspaper since they are not allowed to have televisions. Noah grew up reading Highway Herald and felt safe sharing his own harrowing experiences with this family run newspaper.

He was beseeched by many in his community to not disturb the order of things, but he pushed on and within days of publication, Private Noah Miller was placed under arrest and sent to an undisclosed location for a military trial.

The proverbial cat was out of the proverbial bag and so was the fact, that a young Amish boy, who was taught to cherish human life, saw firsthand how his own countrymen killed, maimed and destroyed that same human dignity.

Congressional hearings were held while the President signed the release of Private Miller on the condition that he help present his case to Congress and cooperate fully with the now civilian investigation of US military conduct in the quaint village of Moo Ban Suay.

One such hearing for Private Noah Millers account of the Moo Ban Suay massacre was two hours from now. My job is to safely transport him to and from the hearing.

"The car is here!" I announced to the small hotel room where both of us were staying for the past week.

"Do you think I am right?" Noah asked as he continued to look at his shoes.

"It doesn't matter," I answered as I looked at the young boy who was dressed in what some might call ‘funeral attire'.

"Then what matters to you?" he retorted as he looked up at me.

"It matters that I keep you safe," I answered calmly, as he continued to look up at me.

"So that you can tell your story!" I added. He got up on his feet and looked me straight in the eye.

"Thank you for helping me!" he said with a broken expression.

"No problem!" I smiled, as I moved in front of him and opened the hotel room door.

It was a silent ride, as we made our way to the US Capitol Building where the hearing was supposed to be held. My head was on a swivel as I looked at every corner and intersection for people willing to teach the young traitor a lesson.

"Hello, my name is Irvin Lee, I am the Chief of Staff for Congressman Quintero" a young man popped up in the foyer, as he welcomed the delegation of guards, in the middle of which stood Private Miller.

"The hearing will start in an hour; we have prepared a special waiting room for you!" he added as we made our way into the Capitol Building.

The room was special indeed. There were no windows (which I appreciated) and there were secondary bunker doors, which would close in case of emergency.

"Lieutenant Freeman, I don't feel so good!" Noah spoke in a soft voice as the door closed behind Lee.

"What is it? Do you need to go to the bathroom?" I asked. Noah nodded as I looked around for a door in the waiting room.

"There is no attached bathroom, in this room, we have to go outside, is that OK with you Noah?" I asked to which Noah nodded again.

"You two, with me!" I ordered two of the guards who stood just behind Noah as we exited the special waiting room.

"This way!" I pointed towards a small subtle signage, that spelled restrooms.

Noah ran towards the restroom, hand on his mouth. He barely dodged the janitor who was exiting the restroom. I chased after him as the spring doors closed behind him. The bathroom was empty, well except for Private Noah who was sitting down on his knees as he retched freely into the open toilet seat.

"There! There!" I patted him on the back. He vomited some more.

After what felt like hours of nauseating sounds, Noah reared his head as he got back up on his feet and washed his hand in the basin opposing the stalls.

"Might as well take a leak, the hearing can go on for hours, you know!" I pointed towards the urinals. There were three separate urinals but only one of them was in working order, the other two were boarded up, for maintenance work.

Noah nodded as he wiped his face with a paper towel and headed towards the working urinal. I moved towards the basin, to wash my hands. I wished I had some disposable gloves, so that I wouldn't have to wash Noah's breakfast off my hands.

"Gloves!" a thought crossed my mind, as I stopped to look at the door. The water ran, as the automatic sensor on the tap blinked red.

In a flashing second, it dawned on me. The Janitor was wearing white gloves. Why was he wearing white gloves? The automatic tap in front of me stopped as the red light on the motion sensor blinked again.

I moved towards Noah and pushed him away from the urinal. The automatic flush light, that activated when the user steps away, turned red again, as a loud shot rang out in the empty bathroom.

A sharp pain travelled up my chest and into my teeth. I crashed onto the cold tile floor as something warm drenched the back of my shirt. I looked up at the sensor, which is used for auto flush. All I saw was a wide hole, made by a bullet, from a specialized weapon that was set behind the sensor, to kill Noah.

Darkness descended upon me as I saw the acne ridden face of Noah, trying to call for help. All I could say to him was —

"*Ulagaththil mighavum marmamaana mozhi ethu*"

* * *

I searched the Scribe's Garb carefully, and I found a Suvarna Gold Coin. Looks standard issue on the first glance, but in my years as a spy I have learnt not to trust first glances.

I felt the coin in my hand, its edges were jagged which means it was minted by one of the Merchant Guilds.

"But which one?" I thought to myself as I turned it over for a closer look. A cross with four circles, recently minted, weighted towards left.

"Senapati!" I mumbled to myself as I ran outside and turned left towards one of the larger tents.

Senapati Dakshata was the Master of Soldiers in the Chakravartin Army, and his tent rose higher than the rest around. The only tent bigger was that of the Emperor himself. As I approached it, sword in one hand the jagged coin in another, the guards on the entrance dropped their spears across to forbid me entry.

"Nayak Bhagwadajjukam, the Senapati is indisposed at the moment!" the guard on the left spoke without looking at me.

"Let me pass, this is a matter of Emperor's Security!" I ordered the left guard as I saw the right one swallow a knot.

"Dakshata!" I called the Master of Soldiers, from across the crossed spears. The two soldiers stepped forward as my palm moved towards the hilt of my sword. There was sudden movement as a hooded figure emerged from the back of Senapati's tent and started running towards the river.

"I knew it!" I mumbled to myself as I pushed the partially unsheathed sword back in my scabbard and broke into a run, in pursuit of the traitor. The two soldiers behind me followed suit.

On a good day, I would have taken both of them, but I needed to stop Dakshata, before he escaped. The hair on the back of my neck stood up, as I lunged left, and a spear flew by me. I soon realized that their intention was to kill and not to wound as I felt another spear fly closer to my head this time. I fully expected Dakshata to turn around, and corner me with his two loyal guards, but the traitorous coward kept on running, holding the neck of his hood and as fast as he can.

"Dakshata!" I roared, as I realized the guards were no longer on my tail and my decision to take off the breastplate had proven useful as a boon of speed allowed me to catch up to the evading traitor.

In a moment, his escape plan became clear. There was a small boat, rocking gently, near the shore. I pushed harder as I held out one hand to grab his billowing robe and other to pull out my sword. I had the edge of his hood in my hand as I tripped on the hem of his robe.

He struggled to push me off, but I held firm and managed to get up on his chest, I punched hard, but instead of meeting the usual scruff of his beard, I met smooth, supple skin. I let go of the bubbling hatred that blinded me and looked at my prisoner, who was now pinned below me.

It was not Dakshata; it was one of his chambermaids. In fact, this one was more than a chambermaid as I had seen her before accompanying the Senapati out on long walks. She was most definitely his mistress, and more importantly his confidant.

"Where is Dakshata?" I asked as I grabbed her by the neck. She turned her neck towards the camp. I followed her gaze, and a sudden realization dawned upon me.

"It's happening now!" I thought to myself as I let go of the traitor woman and broke into another run towards the camp. The two loyal guards were nowhere to be seen. They probably gave up the chase after they used up their weapons as projectiles. I looked at the tree line to the left, as a painful memory washed over me.

"The Emperor!" a clarifying thought pulled me back to reality as I set my eyes at the largest tent in the entire river basin.

After what felt like an eternity, my heart was beating out of my chest as I managed to stop in front of the Emperor's Tent. I caught my breath and started walking towards the ornate entrance. The usual personal guard of the Emperor was ominously missing.

"Where are the guards?" I thought to myself as I stopped in my tracks. I cannot go in from the front. I must maintain my advantage of surprise. I slowly edged towards the back of the tent and pulled out my sword.

I made a small hole in the ornate fabric of the royal tent and peeked inside. To my surprise, there was no one inside except the Emperor, who was gently strolling around the war table. He seemed to be going over the battle plans for the invasion. Suddenly there was movement outside the tent, as multiple soldiers entered the tent followed by the Senapati himself.

"Daksha? What brings you here?" the Emperor asked in his usual calm voice.

"I wish to parlay!" the smug expression on the short but muscular Master of Soldiers' face made my blood churn.

"Parlay?" the Emperor, asked as he looked around at the dozen or so, Mauryan Soldier, who all looked somehow different.

"Yes Parlay! I wish that you go back to the Capital!" the Senapati spoke, with the same air of smugness, as he walked over to the sand war table.

"Who was it?" the Emperor asked calmly, having caught on, that the dozen or so soldiers were there at Dakshata's command and not his.

"Trade and War do not belong together!" Dakshata drew a circle in sand around the port city of Tamralipta.

"The guilds?" the Emperor asked as Dakshata's smug expression turned into a smile.

"Always thinking one step ahead, the Great Chakravartin Samrat!" Dakshata mocked the Emperor's insight.

"I wished you would have found a more loyal master!" the Emperor, turned towards the table as the soldiers all had a clear view of his back. In that moment I saw it. The thing that made the soldiers look a bit different was the armband around their biceps, which bore the same seal of a cross with four circles on each end. They were all bought out by the guilds.

"So what do you say, my lord?" Dakshata asked as he positioned himself at the center of the coup battalion, his back now towards the main entrance. This was my chance.

I pulled away slowly from the hole and looped back to the main entrance. Sword in hand and light-footed, I approached the main entrance as I heard muffled sounds of Senapati's tirade.

"So be it! Seize him!" Dakshata's voice became clear as it echoed around the tent and soldiers moved forward to seize the

Emperor. I contemplated for a moment and lunged at his back in the next, as I drove the sword into his heart.

He gasped as he held on to the blade that now originated from his chest. I turned the blade to make him feel a little bit more pain before his death. The soldiers around the Emperor backed away as I turned the blade some more.

The Emperor, let out a smile as Dakshata collapsed on his knees and I pulled my sword out. I smiled back, only to see his smile fade just a little.

Before I knew it, one of the soldiers behind the Emperor had broken away and plunged his sword into my left side. I looked up at the Emperor, who ordered the scared guild soldiers to seize my attacker.

I fell to my knees as my attacker was wrestled away from me. The tent became darker and darker as I saw the Emperor rush to my aid. Finally the darkness was clear and all I could think was —

"*Ulagaththil mighavum marmamaana mozhi ethu*"

* * *

"My lord, the Nayak is awake!" a voice echoed as I opened my eyes to a middle-aged man, who was wearing a large saffron turban and a magnanimous smile. His skin was dark, yet radiant with a self-satisfied smugness about him.

"Ajju! Can you hear me?" the man with the weird turban inquired. I nodded. He stepped back to reveal himself completely. My eyes opened wider to see the most oddly dressed man that I have ever seen in my life.

Tall, imposing and mysterious, he stood taller than the rest of the people in what looked like a spacious tent. Apart from the turban, he wore an ornate silk draping with gold outlines around his neck, which flowed along his chest and down towards his waist. He also wore what appeared to be ankle high pants, but they weren't exactly pants, it was more like the same silk was wrapped around his legs in cascading folds that disappeared around his waist. As if this wasn't enough, he wore gold all over, and I do mean all over. His neck, his arms, his ankles, even his ears were pierced with textured gold hoops. Was I dreaming or is this some sort of elaborate prank?

"Water!" I spoke instinctively in some language that I had never heard before.

"Here! Veer Nayak!" a shorter man with similar but less ornate clothing replied in the same unknown flowing language. He rushed forward with a black clay pot. The dark surface of the water looked inviting as I lifted my hands up to grab the pot. A sharp pain surged in my abdomen as I grabbed my left side. I felt something slimy, and there it was, the source of my pain. I pulled back my hand and looked at it. It was covered in a transparent paste, that had splotches of red swimming through it.

"It doesn't make sense!" I mumbled to myself. I was shot in my stomach, why am I bleeding from my side.

"The healers wanted to burn the wound shut, but I asked them to sew it in. I might have been wrong about that!" the tall imposing man looked at the blood spots that swam in the cool transparent paste.

"Where am I? What happened to —?" I stopped. The four men in the tent looked at me curiously. I forgot about Noah, the janitor might have doubled back to finish the job. I need to wake up from whatever this is. I need to check on Noah. A wave of shame engulfed my body as I fell back to the hard bedding. The man holding the pot withdrew himself as the tall man drew nearer, once again.

"You were stabbed by one of the guild traitors," the tall man spoke calmly.

"Guild traitors? What do you mean?" I asked the man, as the servant the with water pot coughed.

"Yes, Ajju the guild traitors! They have probably allied themselves with Kalinga, to delay our invasion plans, but we must wait no more. As soon as you have gathered enough strength, we will attack at once and I will take Padmanabhan's head for this insolent conspiracy!" the tall man declared with a hint of anger in his voice. More importantly why must he call me Ajju, who the hell is Ajju? He signaled to the man holding the pot, who came forward at once.

"Drink up and recover! I will talk to the healers and pray for your recovery," he continued. The man with pot stepped forward as I leaned in to drink the water from the dark clay pot, but before I could take a sip, I saw the most horrifying thing of all on the black water surface.

It was not me who looked back in the reflection. It was a darker man, with smoother skin and dark long hair. I pulled back and edged back slowly to look at myself once more. I was still the same.

"For it will be you, who will be replacing Dakshata as my Senapati in the upcoming battle!" the tall man announced as the helpers around him dropped to their knees, pulled out their swords and put them in front.

I looked around helplessly, still unsure as to what was happening. The men bowed deep as their heads touched their blades. Something deep within me felt proud and a nasty smirk appeared on my face.

* * *

"What's beyond the river?" I asked my mother as she washed my grandfather's loincloth on the ghat.

"Kalinga!" she replied as she wiped the sweat off her brow.

"What is Kadinga?" I asked as I threw pebbles into the flowing river.

"Another Kingdom!" she replied as she beat the wet loincloth on the smooth rock.

"*OYE VE OYE*!" a voice came from across the river. I stopped to look at the source, as I picked up a larger, jagged stone.

A whoosh sound broke the silence as I stared at the tree line on the other side of the river.

"Ajju!" I heard my mother call out. I turned around. The white loincloth she was holding was slowly turning red. I looked up at her face. Her hand was on her neck as she gasped for air. It was then that I saw it.

There was an arrow stuck in my mother's throat as a stream of blood trickled down from her neck and on to the smooth stone below her.

My heart was beating fast as I tried to make sense of what just happened as the image of my silently screaming mother dissolved and I opened my eyes.

"Nurse! Nurse!" a man with a face as white as a ghost ran away from me and started calling for someone outside in a peculiar language.

I looked up, as a scorching white light blinded me, and I stared at my hands. They were white too, just like the man who was leaning against the threshold. I had a white bracelet on my arm and a thin red vine that ran from my hand to a suspended red pot. Wait it was not a pot, it looks like an organ. What is this? Where am I? Where is the Emperor?

"Mr. Freeman, how are you feeling? Can you please blink for me!" a dark-skinned man in a white garb entered the room and flashed the same blinding light using a reed like tool.

"Who? Where am I?" I asked as I looked around to find a few more people with the same peculiar garb entering the fray.

"Lieutenant Simeon Freeman, can you remember the time before you got shot?" the dark-skinned man asked me in the same amorphous language.

"I don't!" I replied, somehow in the same language. The dark-skinned man, pressed down on my stomach as a searing pain erupted through my chest.

I looked down to see a white patch on my stomach. I don't remember being stabbed in the stomach. Just then a man entered the room, with two other taller men who were wearing dark robes that hugged the entire length of their body. The man in the middle was shorter and thinner and had the same ghostly white face as the rest of them.

I did not know who this man was, but something deep inside me felt a sense of deep disturbance, as I fell back down into my slumber.

* * *

This is not a dream. I have woken up every single day, groggy and in pain from the stab wound that I cannot remember. I can understand and speak a language that I have never heard before. I am supposed to prepare for a war that I have never signed up for. I am not myself.

I am in a war cantonment which houses the largest army I have ever seen. Something deep within me feels pride when it gazes over the vast river basin, covered with camps and tents up until the horizon.

"Your wound has changed you! You don't speak as much" the Emperor pointed at my stomach as we trotted through the camps, inspecting the soldiers and the bannermen. He looked at me hoping I would say something, but I was too preoccupied with the immense sight in front of me.

A huge elephant, the like of which I had never seen before, was making his way towards me. He had a whole tent setup on his back, in front of which sat a shirtless man with a large spear.

"Mahouti, was born during the time of my grandfather!" the Emperor pointed at the elephant as we sidelined our horses to let the great beast pass.

"He was bred for war on Kalinga, to be waged by my grandfather, but Kalinga never relented in his reign" he continued as the Elephant Mahouti descended into the turbulent waters of the Mahanadi River.

"My father, didn't share my grandfather's ambition and he spent all his life cooped up in comfortable palace chambers, surrounded by his many concubines," he continued some more as we passed a long open tent, where large men covered in soot, were smithing weapons for the army.

"It took me many years and a lot of sacrifices to make sure that my father didn't pass the throne to someone as unambitious as him, and now that I am successful, the time has come for my grandfather's dreams to come true." The Emperor turned around as a small band of soldiers marched past behind him.

"With you at my side as my Senapati, Kalinga WILL fall tomorrow!" he looked deep in my eyes. His intense expression, mixed with kindness and rage ignited something deep inside me.

"Magadha will finally be whole!" he declared as the two soldiers who rode at our wings bowed deeply.

I looked at the riders and realized that I was supposed to bow as well. The expectation in the Emperor's eyes confirmed it. I bowed slowly, though not as deep as the riders.

* * *

I threw the goblet of grey water. I wished it to break into a thousand pieces, but instead it just slumped against the wall and the hot water jumped out of it.

"What kind of goblet doesn't break" I thought to myself as the woman in white backed away and pulled out a dark object from the wall.

"I need help in Room 401" she said with apprehension.

"Where is the Emperor? I wish to see him now!" I screamed at the lady as two white robed men entered the room.

"The patient is having a psychotic episode, push 2 milligrams Haldol" the first man ordered the lady in white.

"What have you done to me?" I asked as I looked at the strings that originated from my body and into something that made a sound every few moments.

"The Haldol is not working" the other robed man said as he flashed something in my eye.

"I need to see the Emperor!" I screamed as the strings that came out of me pulled away and I sat straight up.

"We need to sedate, push B52 and call the staff about some restraints!" the man spoke in his peculiar tongue as the lady in white looked through the wooden post next to my bed. The other man in white held my feet as I was forced into a sedentary position.

"That won't be necessary!" a voice came from behind as all three of my assailers froze.

"Lieutenant Freeman!" the short and thin man in the black garb was back. I stopped struggling.

"You are in charge of security for Private Noah Miller." the man spoke calmly, as something deep inside me, felt a pang of pain.

"Noah?" I mouthed the word.

"Private Miller is okay!" the man confirmed as the pang within me died down.

"You are in the Lincoln Memorial Hospital in Washington DC, you are being treated for the bullet wound you sustained while trying to defend Private Miller!" the man explained further as the white robed men and women backed away. I looked around at the small chamber, with white walls and white skinned people. I looked at my hands, which were also white. I was not myself.

"I will take it from here, you may leave." the mysterious man in dark ordered the three people in my room.

"You took your job too seriously!" the man smiled as he stepped closer to my bed. I looked at him intently. He had dark eyes and cleanly parted shiny hair. He had the same white skin as the other people I have seen so far. His jaw was sharp, and he was a bit shorter than the rest of my captors. Yet there was an aura about him as the people in white had obeyed him unconditionally and without protest.

"You don't speak much, do you?" he taunted me as I looked around some more.

"Where are my manners? I haven't even introduced myself. My name is Joseph Langley, I am from the Agency," the man got up and held out his hand in front of me.

"Agency?" I mumbled as I instinctively pushed my hand forward to meet his.

"I think you know, which Agency I am talking about," he raised his right eyebrow as he tilted his head forward. I did not respond, as he pulled his hand away and turned around.

"Private Noah Miller is a traitor," he said with his back turned, "and you know that!" he turned around. Something felt out of balance as he said those words.

"Miller? How?" I mumbled. I could not remember this Private Miller, but a bond was there, that made me care for whoever he was.

"I don't know what he has told you, but whatever happened in Moo Ban Suay was highly authorized and more importantly, completely justified!" he began. I looked at him confusedly as he let out a sigh.

"Let me start from the top!" he said, as he approached my bedside.

"On the night of the patrol, Captain Everett and his men were acting on a tip by the Agency, to root out the Tiger operatives hiding in Moo Ban Suay!" he sat down on a chair beside my bed. I propped myself up to listen closely.

"Our intelligence was correct! The sympathizers in the village let those operatives escape, and we were left with more questions," he continued as I tried to put the pieces of this unknown puzzle together.

"Captain Everett, in the heat of the moment resorted to enhanced interrogation methods to pry out further intel from the sympathizers, which angered the people of the village!" he stopped to pick up a transparent pail of water and sipped at its surface.

"What happened next was unfortunate, as the locals descended upon them with whatever tools they could find. The only option for Captain Everett and his men was to shoot their way out of there!" he finished with a gulp.

"This Captain Everett you speak of, was he under your command?" I asked in their strange language.

"Not directly, but yes he was working on our intelligence!" the man in black answered without hesitation.

"What happened next?" I decided to push my advantage, as I still felt clueless about this entire situation which might just be a fever dream. I might just wake up back in my tent beside the Mahanadi or I might already be dead, and this reality is the final imagination of a dying mind.

"Well you know what happened!" he hinted as if I already knew the answer. I continued to stare at him without blinking. He looked at me with confusion.

"Private Miller, who was with Captain Everett, came back the next day, illegally broke into the comms building, stole the tapes and made them public. Now the enemies of America are champing at the bits, for revenge! or in their fucked-up language — 'justice'" he raised his voice at the last word.

"So, this Private Miller —" I began my question.

"— is a goddamn traitor!" he interrupted me as an image of Dakshata, flashed in my mind, "and you know it!" he concluded.

There was silence in the room. I tried to digest the information I just heard. This Private Miller betrayed his country, and he is allowed to walk free. I felt an intense rage as my thoughts drifted back to Senapati Dakshata and his traitorous ways.

"The urinal assassination was a foolish idea, concocted by the simpler minds at the Agency!" he began again as I saw someone near the small see-through window in the door. I turned my head to get a better look, but the face had vanished.

"But the failed plan, although unfortunate has given me some face time with you!" he pointed at my stomach as a sharp pain ran through my upper body. I distinctly remember being stabbed in my side so why was the pain coming from my gut.

"You were my plan from day one. You are assigned to Private Miller's Personal Security Detail, and I want you to take him down, before he gives our enemies more reasons to cheer for our demise," he pointed both of his hands at me.

There was a loud crashing sound that came from the other side of the door. The man called Langley turned around to see who it was. The door remained unopened.

"I must leave now. Think about what I said. I will be in touch!" he spoke with intensity as he walked back to the door. I continued to digest the twisted truth that had just been set upon me like a wild beast.

Meanwhile he opened the door, peeked outside and looked both ways.

"So long Lieutenant Freeman!" he turned around and let out a sinister smile as he disappeared behind the closing door.

* * *

A large army of disparate banners and equally different uniforms gathered over the horizon. On the other side, soldiers dressed in standard brown colors, with their generals wearing maroon hued tunics gathered on the north end of the Mahanadi River.

I wore the same maroon, with flashes of deep red as I trotted along the frontline inspecting the spear heights of the foot soldiers and the bow placements of the riders beside them.

Behind the front line stood five large War Elephants, Mahouti being the one in front. The tent above him was now occupied by archers and men with loud trumpets. Infront of Mahouti was a distinct dark horse atop which rode the gold armored Chakravartin Samrat Emperor Ashoka.

I felt off about his choice of armor, which made him standout from the sea of brown and red of the mighty Mauryan Army. But then again, they don't have snipers in this day and age, so I guess his armor only inspires morale.

His equal on the other side was also visible, albeit less impressive, King Padmanabhan of Kalinga had arrived on the battlefield, with mostly silver strung armor with a bit of gold in it, he stood behind his frontline, in an ornate chariot pulled along by two handsome white horses.

Ashoka cantered forward on his dark horse and stopped beside me. I looked at him and gave a reluctant bow. He let out a kind smile and turned around as he pulled out his ornate silver blade.

"Their existence has insulted our presence for too long!" the Emperor's voice boomed across the river basin as he pointed his blade towards the Kalingan Army.

"They tricked Chandragupta and waged war on our borders for years!" he continued as I looked at the attentive army.

"Your own Senapati Bhagwadajjukam, lost his mother to their treachery!" he pointed his blade towards me. Something deep inside me felt a pang of passing pain.

"Today they will answer for their crimes! Today Magadha will be victorious and tonight Kalinga will fall!" he raised his swords as war chants erupted across the basin. The rider with the large spear on Mahouti jammed the spear into the elephant's side as it let out deafening roar. I turned around to look at the Kalingan Army. To my surprise there was no fear on their faces. They were still resolute, and their King still looked on with confidence as the Magadha War chants filled the battleground.

"Ajju! you have the command!" the Emperor spoke softly as I stepped forward.

"Archers! Ready!" I bellowed as the line of archers on the ground and atop the horses pulled arrows from their quivers.

"Knock!" I commanded as they knocked the arrow and pointed it towards the sky.

"LOOSE!" I screamed as the sky turned dark and the battle for Kalinga finally started.

The next few hours were hazy to say the least. Something deep inside me took over as I shouted commands at the generals and the riders. After a dozen exchanges of arrowing rain, the battle moved into its combat mode, as the Magadha frontline collided with the ragtag frontline of Kalinga.

I rode in the vanguard taking down multiple riders who intended to disturb the spear vanguard that was now splitting the Kalinga army in two.

"Avesu!" a general to my left roared as a dark red flag rose up to my right. Four more units of the Mauryan army were now flanking the two halves of Kalinga.

As we dove deeper and deeper the soldiers became sparse, until we had finally made it to the back. I turned around to see the four units engulfing, what was left of the Kalingan soldiers.

"Padmanabhan is on the run!" the general cried out as a silver light flashed atop the hill. It was Padmanabhan's Chariot, covered on all sides with a small unit of soldiers.

Our goal was to capture Padmanabhan and end this battle quickly. I turned back to see thousands of dead soldiers crying in agony and lying in death. Our best chance was to capture the King, so I decided to beeline for him.

"To me!" I ordered the vanguard unit as the Chariot and it's small guard unit disappeared over the hill.

Our horses climbed the hill with little difficulty as I looked down into the valley and across the horizon for Padmanabhan's silver Chariot. But to my surprise, the valley was not what I expected.

Beyond the river plains and the small hillocks, in this valley laid a small village outside of which were pitched thousands of tents bearing the Kalingan flag.

At once I realized the Kalingan army was probably camped out here as they used the small village for its resources. My eyes travelled up the valley and across the village as I finally spotted Padmanabhan who now stood on the other side. Between me and Padmanabhan stood this small settlement, still teeming with civilians.

"This must be the town of Kalinganagara" the general to my right remarked.

"What are you waiting for, Ajju?" a voice called out to me as I turned around. Through the open corridor secured on both sides by Magadha riders, came a dark horse atop which rode the Emperor.

"The village has not been evacuated, my lord" I presented my dilemma to the Emperor.

"So what?" he looked at me with confusion.

"To get to Padmanabhan we have to go through the village," I continued hoping we were on the same page.

"If Padmanabhan escapes Kalinga will never be a part of Magadha!" he justified the attack on the small settlement.

"But my lord —" I protested.

"This is no time for weakness, relinquish your post!" he interrupted me as his horse moved forward and looked up at the hill where Padmanabhan's chariot waited mockingly.

"Onward!" the Emperor pulled out his sword as the whole army turned towards him.

A wave of brown and red descended into the valley as I rode behind them, trying to keep up. Civilians emerged from their houses and tried to make for the opposing hill where Padmanabhan waited with a tense expression on his face. A hail of arrows from his small unit halted their ascent. They turned back towards the incoming Mauryan army. The onslaught began as time slowed down. The residents of Kalinganagara were massacred one by one as they found themselves trapped between two tyrants.

"This is what he is, A tyrant!" a realization dawned upon me.

He is no better than Padmanabhan. He is just another power-hungry warlord. I pulled out my sword and charged towards the dark horse that carried the gold armored Emperor.

"If I kill him, this massacre will stop!" I thought to myself as I made my way through the genocidal Mauryan Army. He was guarded by the same general who accompanied me in the vanguard. He stood at the edge of the town. If only I can get to him faster.

It all happened in an instant as a rider hit me on my broadside as I flew off my horse and thrashed on the ground. Another rider passed by as an arrow impaled him in his chest and he crashed right on top of me. The wind in my lungs left me as darkness descended all around me.

"*Āvi tirumpuka*" a voice called out to me as I opened my eyes and water rushed into my eyelids. I was underwater holding my breath. I looked around to get my bearings. There was a soldier in the driver's seat who was unconscious, and I could feel two more in the back who were not responding. As I turned back to confirm, my heart sank.

Diagonally opposite to my seat, lay the unconscious body of Private Noah Miller. I looked around to see where I was. I was definitely underwater trapped in a drowning car.

I pulled out my Karambit knife and cut away the seat belt. I turned the knife around and rammed the hilt into the glass. Nothing happened. I hit it again as a crack appeared on the window glass. I hit it one final time as more water rushed into the car, breaking away the plate glass. I wrestled my way out through the window and swam up towards the surface as I saw the sunlight and the water get warmer and warmer.

I broke the surface and gasped for a fresh breath. It finally came as the warm air filled my lungs and I realized what was drowning beneath my feet. I was no longer on the battlefield charging towards a Tyrant Emperor, I was back in my own body as Lieutenant Simeon Freeman. But something has gone horribly wrong in my absence, as I looked around to see if there were any rescue teams approaching the scene.

There were only onlookers from the bridge at a distance, the side of which was completely destroyed by something heavy. I took in a deep breath and dived again.

The black SUV was drowning deeper and deeper with each passing second. As I approached the broken glass, I saw the driver struggling with his seat belt. He was finally awake. I made my way into the car and cut away his seatbelt. He rushed past me towards the window, and I saw him swim up to the surface. The soldier in the back and Noah were still unconscious. I made my way in the back of the car as a metallic taste flooded my mouth.

It was blood. It was coming from somewhere. My heart sank some more as I checked Noah's body for puncture wounds. There were none, which means the blood was coming from the soldier. I checked his body and sure enough I found it. A piece of white bridge railing had penetrated his back side, cutting open his spine. His heart was no longer beating. I let out a little air, as I saw the white railing remerge from the back of his neck.

Suppressing an urge to vomit, I turned my attention towards Noah as I cut his seat belt and pulled him towards my broken window. I could feel his feeble heartbeat through the pulse in his scrawny arms. I pulled and pulled as both of us came out of the car. There was darkness descending around my vision as I pulled Noah and tried to swim to the surface.

But his leg was stuck in the seatbelt that I cut for myself. He was pulling me down as the car pulled him in return. The darkness became more prominent as my vision shrank to a small pinpoint. I had failed in my mission to protect the innocent Amish boy from Indiana. I had broken my promise. I am nothing —

Warm air rushed into my lungs as I coughed water onto the muddy shores of the river. I looked up to see the soldier that I freed earlier dragging me out of the water. My hand was still gripped tight around something.

It was Noah, I didn't let go. I turned around to pull the young Private out of the water. He was not breathing. I jerked myself free from the soldier's grip as I turned around to give CPR to the young Noah. I placed him flat on the grass near the shore, and started compressing his chest, occasionally putting my head onto his chest to listen for normal breathing. I opened his mouth and blew into his airways as I pulled up to do the compressions again.

Water bubbled from his mouth, and he started coughing.

"Lieuten— ant" he mumbled as I smiled widely, thanking God in my heart for having saved him.

"Lieutenant Simeon Freeman!" another voice came from above. I looked up to see the soldier that I rescued pointing a gun at me.

"You are under arrest for endangering the life of a public witness!" he announced as I looked around to confirm that there wasn't another Simeon Freeman that he was talking to.

* * *

"I wished you would have made better use of the knowledge I gave you" the voice spoke in condescension.

* * *

"Lieutenant Freeman, you are alright!" a young man in a full uniform smiled as I stepped out of the dark vehicle.

"I am —" the young man hugged me before I could finish my sentence. I looked at him intently as I ran my eyes through what he was wearing. A dark green garb, with pockets on each side and a belt that tightened the garb around his waist. He also wore a cap, unlike anything I had ever seen. Atop the hat sat a gold insignia of a large ferocious bird. On his left breast was a small black plaque that said —

"Private Miller! Your hearing has been moved from the Capitol" a soldier wearing patched camouflage spoke up, "it is to be held at the Annapolis State House, now!" I turned around to look at him and his compatriot guarding the car.

"Annapolis? How far is it?" Miller asked as I looked back at the young man. This is the supposed traitor, the one who has betrayed his country. How can someone so young, even think of going against his own. An image of my mother flashed in my mind. She held her throat as she tried to pull out the arrow that ran across it. I dismissed the image and looked back at the traitor.

"The river, not the lake!" I mumbled to myself as Miller turned his attention back towards me.

"Did you say something Lieutenant?" he asked, perplexed. I shook my head.

"We must go; we are running late!" the other soldier announced as I made way for the young man to get into the dark vehicle. I sat in the front, the same seat that I rode in on.

"Your seat belt lieutenant!" the soldier on my left who sat in front of the ring announced. My hand moved instinctively across my chest and pulled out a belt which ran back across my chest as a click indicated that the 'seat belt' was in position.

"How do you feel, Lieutenant?" the young man asked me, as he put a hand on my soldier.

"I feel good!" I dropped my shoulders, and his hand slipped off me. The hate that I had for the traitor didn't seem right, somehow. Was the man in black telling the truth? Is what I am about to do, justified?

The young man slinked back into his backseat, a little scorned as I felt his eyes penetrate the side of my face. I was the only one who was dressed in the same dark garb as the man in black. I think it's time.

"Kingman Lake?" I asked the soldier to my left.

"Did you say something Lieutenant?" the soldier asked as he leaned his head towards me.

"Kingman Lake, how far is it?" I asked hoping to get an answer without suspicion.

"We will pass over the lake on our way out of DC." he informed me, "Why do you ask, Lieutenant?" the soldier added a question.

"I always wanted to see it!" I lied, as the young man looked away from the window and fixed his gaze back towards me.

"All these years in the capital and you have never seen the Kingman Lake, Lieutenant?" the soldier smiled as I heard a chuckle from the back. It was the other soldier.

"I don't need your questions! Just tell me when we are near!" I commanded sternly as the soldier stiffened up.

"Understood Sir!" he cleared his throat.

"The river, not the lake!" that's what the man in black said when he told me his plan to kill the traitor. He asked me to take over the vehicle near the Young Memorial Bridge which spans over Kingman Lake and Anacostia River. I am supposed to 'crash' the vehicle so that it flies off the bridge and into the river.

There will be agents waiting near the bridge, who will pull me out and make sure there are no survivors. The whole thing would look like an accident and all of us will be assumed dead. Due to the flow of the river my body will never be found, giving me the perfect cover to take on a new identity.

Something deep within me, doesn't feel right, but all I know is that young man has betrayed his country and dishonored his people. Just like Dakshata, he must also meet his end. Multiple conflicting thoughts crossed my mind, as the vehicle took off.

"We are nearing the lake now; do you want me to slow down? “I know we cannot stop—" the soldier reported as we turned right. I could feel the vehicle climbing that means we must be on a hill. A large rusting structure rose to my left.

"This must be the 'stadium' Langley was talking about!" I thought to myself as a tree line to my right started thinning out.

"Sir! Do you want me to slow down?" the soldier asked again.

"No! Keep going!" I answered as I kept looking out the window for the sign of a lake.

"There!" I thought to myself as I saw what looked like a wide river, with stagnant water.

This means the river must be just a few steps away. And there it was again, the same size as the lake, but with flowing turbulent waters. I turned towards the soldier and looked back at the young man who was still looking out the window at the passing lake. I grabbed the ring that the soldier used to control the vehicle and pulled it towards me.

"LIEUTENANT? WHAT THE —" the soldier screamed as he tried to take back control, but it was too late.

The vehicle swerved and crashed into the iron rails to my side. They broke easily as the vehicle floated in the air for a moment and then with a deafening noise hit the surface of the river.

"*Āvi tirumpuka*" a voice from outside called out to me as I opened my eyes. There was something or someone pressing against my chest. I pushed the body aside to see a dark sky.

My hand closed around the sword as I pulled myself up. I was on a battlefield. A battlefield of my own time. I was wearing my armor. I am myself again. Waves of joy surged through my being as I looked around to see the ground singed with blood and bodies for as far as the eye can see.

"Get away from me!" a feminine voice broke the eerie silence. I looked in the direction of the sound. In the distance a dark figure was descending upon a crying woman.

"You killed my child! Get away from me!" she screamed again as the dark figure stepped closer and closer. I propped myself up with my sword and rushed to the woman's aid.

"Murderer!" she screamed again as I raised my sword to attack the dark figure. It turned around just in time, as I halted my attack. My body overcame in fear and awe as I threw down my sword and fell to my knees.

"Emperor, it is you!" I joined my hands in prayer, as I looked at my lord's visage.

"Murderer!" she screamed again from behind as a gasp originated from my mouth.

The Emperor eyes were full of tears and his expression that of shame. The woman behind him must surely be responsible for this. I picked up my sword and got up to confront the insolent wench.

"Let her be!" my Lord roared in a broken voice, as I raised my sword. I stopped to look back at him.

"Her life is all she has left for I have taken everything else" he said, in deep remorse as he turned around and started walking back towards the river.

The Emperor has changed.

* * *

"Eidolons are illegal under Mandib law, but I think you already know that!" Adar's voice echoed in the caldera as I opened my eyes.

"Don't you General Zios?" Ada stood before me, having aged not even a moment since I met him in that cave on Solus.

"I am not a General anymore!" I replied as I unfolded my legs and stood up with the help of my rear arms, facing an old friend.

"But you were controlling two soldiers from different times, isn't that what Generals do?" Ada smiled as he walked around me, trying to grab onto something that wasn't there.

"I have been observing your newfound penchant for Voyeurism, especially for the residents of this Planet!" he began his rant.

"What can I say? I like stories." I smirked, watching his rear arms twitch—ready to strike.

"But you tried to rewrite that last story! Didn't you?" Ada snapped back. I remained silent.

"What was your plan exactly? I wish to know," he spoke as his hand touched something invisible. The Lightship broke camouflage and hovered into view.

"Let me guess, you thought if you could switch the consciousness of two soldiers, with completely opposing world views you might be able to change the course of history?" he posited as the ganglia on my neck stood up to predict incoming danger.

"You thought that Lieutenant Simeon would kill the Emperor after recognizing him for the tyrant that he was and half the Earth would change course?" he continued as he walked around the Lightship to find a way to get inside. I sensed something move above me, was Ada alone or did he bring some backup.

"Nayak Bhagwadajjukam, a fierce loyalist would kill Private Miller and change the course of history yet again?" he concluded as he finally found the switch. He pressed it and a large ramp descended into the base of the cold and dark caldera, where the ship was parked. He stepped inside. I looked up at the clear night sky as Earth's Candran that they locally call 'Moon' shone brightly and illuminated the caldera's rim.

"Aren't you coming in?" Ada peeked back out to invite me into my own Lightship. The best thing to do right now is entertain, and that's what I did as I followed him into my stolen Imperial Lightship.

"You know I can just read your thoughts, right?" Ada smiled as I entered the cargo bay. I frowned at the notion.

"So if you don't want me to do that? Just tell me why did you conjure up Eidolons and made them switch places at two different points in time?" he asked again.

"Devon!" I spoke for the first time.

"What about him?" Ada asked.

"I want to kill Devon!" I answered.

"You want to kill the founder of your religion?" Ada raised his eyes.

"Yes!" I said with insolence.

"So you decided to conduct an experiment here on Earth?" Ada asked again to which I just nodded.

"You do know that if you kill Devon, any idea of you will cease to exist. You will have to live outside time, detached from any reality that you once called your own." Ada stepped closer.

"I know the risks!" I answered.

"Then why? Why would you risk losing your mind for some insignificant Mandib that lived and peddled a hardheaded ideology, in the distant past?" he sounded almost sympathetic.

"The schism that resulted from the exodus of the Devant cost us everything!" I began my explanation as Ada tilted his head to absorb my justification.

"Solus is destroyed and the Devant Imperium continues to live in ignorance under my brother's rule!" I continued.

"So conjure an Eidolon and kill your brother. After all he was the one who gathered the Second Sons and financed the invasion of Solus," Ada proposed.

"That was my original plan, but it was guided more by rage than rationality. Killing my brother will still leave Trimecans of Mandib without a direction. They will still follow a false religion that teaches ignorance and violence, forcing them to suppress the voices inside their heads" I shot down his proposal.

"So you want to go back all the way to Devon?" Ada repeated his earlier question.

"Yes! I do. No Devon, no Devant and Trimecan of Sols worth of combined prosperity for the Xaracem and the exiled Devants" I answered.

"You know why Eidolons are outlawed in Mandib common law?" Ada asked. I knew the answer, but I stayed silent.

"To detach somebody from their body, is to take away their souls, their sense of self. It is worse than death, if the soul isn't restored in time!" Ada continued in a tone, which bordered on preaching. I scoffed.

"But I have to give it to you, nobody tried Eidolency across time!" Ada smiled again.

"What does it matter? You switched them back, before the critical event!" I taunted the wise old Mandib, for foiling my plan.

"Well! It must be hard for you to believe but Mandib Law still exists in this world, even if there is only one Mandib left to enforce it" Ada smiled once again.

"What are you gonna do? Kill me?" I scoffed as I turned around to confirm that Ada hadn't brought reinforcements.

"No! My dear Zios, I am going to do to you, what you did to those two poor soldiers!" his expression turned as I extended my rear arms, to counter, but I was too late. Within a blink of an eye, I was snatched away from my corporeal self, now travelling at greater and greater speeds away from my Lightship.

* * *

"Before you begin your repentance, I wish to show you the aftermath of your careless actions" a voice spoke within me as I tried to grasp the darkness around me.

Suddenly there was light, I was looking down from a podium at a teary eyed but still confident Noah Miller as he rubbed his hands together. I soon realized that I was looking at the Moo Ban Suay Massacre Hearings. Not only was I looking at it, I was the one who was conducting it.

"What did Captain Everett ask you to do once you set fire to the houses?" a voice that was not mine asked the scared young Private.

"He asked us to find and kill the witnesses hiding in the fields!" Noah replied as a man sat in the back, held in place with handcuffs and a security guard. It was Simeon Freeman.

Darkness descended again as I tried to speak but nothing came out.

My eyes opened again as I stood on a hill with violent winds that blew puffs of hair in my face.

Hundreds of men sat on the ground in front of me as bald men shaved the heads to the new recruits. At the front sat the two men I had come to know better in my meditations.

The Chakravartin Samrat Emperor Ashoka and his loyal Senapati Bhagwadajjukam were both taking the vow of Buddhist monkhood as it all went dark again.

"All of your actions were for nothing and now you will repent until you feel remorse" the same voice from before spoke.

We had stopped moving and there was an eerie silence that made me realize that the voice had left me, and I was finally alone.

I tried to scream, but once again, nothing came out.

* * *

Lieutenant Simeon Freeman dishonorably discharged and at nearly 60 years of age lived in a small, secluded cabin on the outskirts of Anchorage, Alaska.

As he packed for his lone fishing trip to Aniakchak, he looked at the hundreds of photos that hung on the cheap wallpaper of his cozy cabin. In these photos he saw himself with his old special ops team, him locked in a heartfelt embrace with the love of his life that he lost because of his own stupidity and finally a duet portrait of two men with their hands on each other's shoulders smiling widely.

Beneath the last photo was a small inscription that read — 'Thanks for saving my life - Signed Dr. Noah Miller'

A sense of pride washed over him as he stepped out of his cabin and called a cab to the local airstrip.

Hours later he was flying on a seaplane he chartered from Port Heiden over the majestic Mount Aniakchak. The weather was clear, and his landing spot shined bright green below him.

The Emerald Green Surprise Lake beside the Aniakchak Crater was one of the hardest places to get to, let alone to fish from, in the whole wide world. Simeon, who was known for his lone wolf demeanor, always cherished the quiet and peace of mind that fishing offered. Pair all that with a secluded lake, nothing could have been closer to heaven.

The white seaplane, piloted solely by Simeon, touched down on the serene lake as jets of cold lake water hit the back of the plane. He turned off the engine and moved to the back, where he had stowed most of his fishing gear along with a small kayak and a small paddle.

Moments later, the kayak had splashed down into the water and Simeon had cast his first bait, with a small herring at the end.

The lake was so clear that the sockeye salmon was clearly visible, as it swam towards the small herring bait.

Simeon played with the fish, as it needed a bit more convincing that the dead herring was still alive. After what felt like timeless bliss, the fish finally took the bait, and Simeon reeled it in for the first catch of the day. The fish looked nice and juicy with his red underbelly and silver mouth. Simeon's stomach rumbled as he dropped the fish in the bucket and headed for the shore.

He pulled the Kayak in as he stepped on solid ground. It was time for him to cook his catch. He pulled out the fish and laid it out on a flat stone. But before he could pull out his knife set, he heard a rustling voice in his head. He looked up at the caldera that neighbored the lake.

There was something on the other side that was calling him. He dropped his tools and picked up his backpack as he started climbing the caldera. The ground became softer and softer with volcanic ash as he approached the rim of the caldera.

Something sparkled in the middle of the caldera, as he made his way over the rim. Just like his climb, he made his way down into the caldera, as he tried to position himself again and again in the direction of the sparkling object.

Once he reached the point where the sparkle came from, he felt a pang of disappointment at the absolute nothingness that surrounded him in this open plane. He cursed himself for being paranoid and decided to hike back up to his kayak.

He has been feeling this kind of paranoia for months now. Ever since he was released from jail, his mind has pulled him closer and closer to this part of the world. In the depths of his being he knew that this was the origin point of that desire. He looped around a small rock formation and headed back, but before he could move in the direction of the climb, he ran into something. Something invisible, which was now taking shape right before his eyes.

An immense silver ship, with blindingly reflective surface stood before him with its backway open. Simeon stood back up and walked around the silver ship, inspecting it from each side.

Finally, he made his way to the open backway. The rustling voice in his head grew louder as he stepped inside. His pulse quickened as he made his way deeper into this seemingly abandoned ship.

There was someone inside the ship, standing waiting for him. He walked forwards as he moved in for a closer look. He stumbled onto something as he tripped against the unknown obstacle. Bending over to inspect, he looked at his own reflection in a large black slab.

But there was something else in the reflection, something that stood behind him, watching him hungrily, with its four arms extended, waiting for him to pick up the slab and hold it until the return of its master.

The auxiliary engines came to life shortly as the inertia pushed me back in my seat.

AFTERWORD

The idea for 'HIVE' came from an earlier concept called 'Celestial Painter'. In this concept world, an 'extra-terrestrial artist' is forced to spend eternity in a lonely castle at the center of an isolated blackhole. His only pastime was to paint these vast murals of stories that he is able to observe unfolding across the universe. Initially, the artist was supposed to be this silent narrator, who would observe and recount these magical stories from his castle as he paints them without bias.

This idea of painting stories as an innocent bystander appealed to me, since it mimicked real life where you are too powerless to stop bad things from happening. I was hell bent on writing my first short story collection under this banner of 'Celestial Painter' until I published my first book 'Shepherd'.

The act of pushing through and being able to tell the story that I had only been able to tell a select few around me, made me realize that you don't have to be an innocent bystander. Publishing 'Shepherd' helped me recognize that you don't have to wait for the right opportunity to fall into your lap, you can and should take control of your destiny, and reshape the reality that you are forced to live within, day after day. I was finally able to do what I really wanted — 'telling stories'

Hence the idea of an active narrator was born. Zios or General Zios for those who have not made it past Chapter 1, was forged in my own ability to affect life. He learns from the stories he tells and is able to take control of his destiny by reshaping some of those stories. The identity of the Celestial Painter still lives on within him, but he becomes an active part of the narrative as he pushes that paintbrush just a little more than required and takes control of the story, across space and time.

With more volumes of HIVE to come, I hope to extend this little box of recollections that Zios is yet to experience. Some stories are told in full, while some still await their deserving endings. This is the true beauty of it all, as I firmly believe that stories are living beings that are born with the turn of a first page and die when lengthy 'AFTERWORDS' like this one, are finally written.

Thank you for reading HIVE Volume 1. I hope to meet you in my future works. Until then enjoy this amateur painting of the Imperial Warship Atreus approaching Mount Amperia in Chapter 1 - The 'Second Son'.

– AMAN (aman@monastichill.com)

OTHER WORKS BY AMAN

SHEPHERD

www.ingramcontent.com/pod-product-compliance
Ingram Content Group UK Ltd.
Pitfield, Milton Keynes, MK11 3LW, UK
UKHW041313190726
13845UKWH00025B/238

9 788198 245489